McCracken County Public Library

3 0002 00100 3045

D0945218

DISCARD

Property of

McCracken County Public Library

555 Washington Street

Paducah, KY 42003-1735

DISCARD

HE RODE ALONE

As a boy he had a look of gaunt horror about him.

As a man he had the cold look of the eternal searcher.

The boy walked out of the wilderness in the late summer of 1855. He had been alone in there for ten days.

Behind him he had left three graves. With him always was the memory of a family named Snelling, that he would one day hunt down and destroy—slowly, terribly.

The boy became a man, bleak-eyed and dangerous, a man named Ed Cushman who rode, always alone, carrying only the grim comfort of a black memory. Searching, always searching.

Murder lay at the end of his trail. Murder and a girl he loved.

HE RODE ALONE

Steve Frazee

This hardback edition 2001
by Chivers Press
by arrangement with
Golden West Literary Agency

Copyright © 1956 by Steve Frazee
Copyright © renewed 1984 by Steve Frazee

All rights reserved

ISBN 0 7540 8126 5

British Library Cataloguing in Publication Data available

Printed and bound in Great Britain by
Redwood Books, Trowbridge, Wiltshire

CHAPTER ONE

THE PLACE was Gravelly Crossing on the Humboldt River, in the late summer of 1855. On the left of the two wagons encamped there, barren mountains stood as bleak as old remembered sins. Grasses reaching out from the brackish river were brown. The sun was hot now, but early in the morning there had been a light frost on the ground and cooking fires had lifted quickly into the haze.

In the second wagon two people were dying.

The second wagon was a tottering, sun-twisted wreck, and because of it passage across the salt desert had been deathly slow. Winter might be two months away, but it was a worse threat than the present heat, for the Forty Mile Desert was still somewhere ahead, and beyond that was the terrible barrier of the Sierras. The dream of warmth and greenness in a land where great blue rivers ran to the sea was hard to hold; it was so far away.

How far away, Eddie Cushman did not know. Time and distance had no meaning. There was only today. He could remember things that had happened when his parents and Kathy and he were traveling in the big, well-ordered train that they had parted with at Fort Hall; but it was now impossible to place the events in order of time.

He was, however, sure of much that had taken place since the Snellings attached themselves to the Cushmans at Fort Hall. The salt desert had been unmitigated hell.

When the two wagons reached the trading post in Ruby Valley, Eddie's father said they were several weeks behind time, but that it was nothing to fret about; they would make it. Ashley Cushman was a calm, good-natured man of tremendous strength both of spirit and body. He gave freely of his strength, and he overlooked the worst in people, even the shiftlessness of the Snellings who were, said Mrs. Cushman, the only people in the world who could have gone so far toward California on borrowed substance.

"Now, Rachel," Ashley said, "you know we got to help them. Look at that bunch of kids."

"I have, and there's only one in the whole litter that I can abide, not counting the baby." Mrs. Cushman was sharp, but she went ahead and doled out food from her own supplies to the Snellings. The Snellings were always grateful. They were going to pay everything back with interest when they reached California, where Rumsey, the fountainhead, had kin who were doing well.

These were the people of the two wagons. It was Ashley Cushman and his wife Rachel who lay sick unto death under the bleached top of their wagon.

. With his arm around Kathy, Eddie tried to bear his thoughts on the green land far ahead, the place of promise, the goal his father had sought. In the dream there must be strength that could be forced inside the wagon where Eddie's parents were unconscious with cholera, attended by Mrs. Snelling. It would be like breaking a promise if Eddie's parents did not get well. Both of them had been so sure of the dream. If there were some way Eddie could make them remember it, then maybe they would have strength to turn aside the sickness and get well.

It was childish, Eddie realized. It was like thinking something good was bound to happen if you took only so many steps between rocks beside the trail; like thinking the tire on the worst rear wheel of Rumsey Snelling's wagon would not come loose again if you stared hard at it and dared it to; it was like watching a bird high in the sky and telling yourself that if it flew west before it flew east, there would be something good for supper that night.

Eddie Cushman was thirteen. Kathy was ten. They stood together some distance from the wagon, waiting for Mrs. Snelling to stick her head out and tell them that everything was all right.

Mrs. Snelling had been quiet for a long time. Death makes its own hush. The forlorn land was quiet. Resting in the shade of their wagon, the Snellings for once were not a noisy, whining lot. Rumsey Snelling sat with his back against a tattered roll of bedding, his loose-knuckled hands hanging between his knees, his hat pulled down so that most of his face appeared to be filthy beard.

He seemed to be asleep, but now and then he spat tobacco juice without raising his head. The three older boys, Reed and John and Jefferson, were sprawled close to him. The five younger boys, all within a few years of Eddie's age, were scratching in the dirt near one of the leaning front wheels. There were only two girls. One was a baby, born during the second week after the Snellings left Independence. Elizabeth was holding her, sitting straight-backed on the ground, staring down toward the river.

If one of the Snellings was different, it was Lizzie. Eddie's mother had said if you met one of them on a dark night in the middle of a river, you'd know at a glance it was a Snelling. They were a roundheaded lot, with thin lips and small noses without any particular bony structure. All the boys, from Reed on down, had a certain boldness of eyes when first met, but a steady look always made them shift their glances, and then they would look back covertly when your attention changed.

Except for Lizzie and the baby, too young to tell about, the Snellings were cast in the mold of the father. Lizzie's eyes were straight-looking and stayed that way when she was talking to you. Her hair was brown, like her mother's, instead of mousy-looking like Rumsey's and the boys'. For a twelve-year-old, her tongue was nasty sharp sometimes, and when she was standing off her brothers in a quarrel she used language as foul as theirs.

She was different from the rest of the tribe, yes; but Eddie was not greatly concerned beyond noticing the fact. They were all a shiftless lot and they had fastened like leeches upon the generosity of Ashley Cushman. Otherwise, the Cushmans would be far down the Humboldt now, and most likely would have overtaken the train which had left Fort Hall a week before the Cushmans arrived there.

The Snellings were a curse. Eddie stared at them with blind anger. The older boys looked back boldly, shifting their eyes after a time. Rumsey spat on the ground between his legs, some of the spittle hanging in his beard. Lizzie sat with the baby in her lap, staring out across the sere grasses.

There was the river, slow in the sun. It was a long lifeline of emigrant travel, but like the other rivers of this forsaken land, it ran only to sink into the earth at last.

Fearing the long silence in the wagon, Eddie forgot the Snellings and tried to resume his prayer: if only his parents would remember all the fine things they had said about California, then everything might be all right.

Snelling raised his head and drawled, "You mought as well set down in the shade, Eddie boy." All the Snelling males looked briefly at their father and it was like the pricking up of ears among a coyote pack when a leader speaks.

Eddie sat down where he was. Kathy pushed over against him and they waited.

John Snelling said, "You reckon they're both dead by now, Pa?"

"You shut up," the father said.

"There ain't been no groans or nothing for a while, and Ma—"

"Shut your mouth. You weary me."

Terror jumped in Kathy's eyes. "He's lying, ain't he, Eddie? John's lying. They won't die, will they?"

Eddie started to say that of course they wouldn't die but he put his arm around Kathy instead and said nothing, for the terror was in him too. Mystic thinking was no longer a support. He had learned hard truths on the long haul. The westward trails were marked with graves of both the weak and the strong. His mother and father had been bad sick for three days. Since the middle of the morning they had been unconscious.

Even *they* could die.

California . . . Eddie had never seen it; he could no longer hold it as a dream to be projected into the wagon to help his parents. The weather-whitened top of the wagon was small against the immenseness of the land. The land had no feeling; it had been there forever, baking in the sun, brutal and unfeeling.

For months the very sight of the wagon had been security itself, because his parents had always been close to it. He remembered his father double-teaming the heavy grades, slow and easy, giving encouragement to the oxen, then going back to help the next wagon. He remembered his father riding back after looking at the trail ahead, big and sure. Even on the salt desert where the Snellings were always having trouble with their wagon, Eddie's father had never lost either his confidence or his temper.

There he would be, making repairs, talking quietly, while the Snellings stood around and whined at their bad luck. Even now it seemed possible that Ashley Cushman could walk around the wagon and stand for a moment as he wiped dust off his forehead with his sleeve, and ask, "What seems to be the trouble here?"

There had been long stretches where the trail was level and easy. Eddie's mother had driven much of that, with Kathy on the seat beside her. Coming in from his chore of helping herd the spare oxen, Eddie would hear them talking as he got a drink from one of the barrels, or maybe Mrs. Cushman would be singing one of the old songs. No matter how choking the dust was back with the loose oxen, or how hot his feet were from plodding along, Eddie would know that everything was all right at the wagon and he would return to his chore without his mother or sister ever knowing that he had been so close. . . .

The silence inside now was terrible.

"Cholera generally kills them before this," John said. He scrabbled out from under the Snelling wagon and rose, scratching his buttocks. "I'm tired of waiting around." He went slouching toward the river.

"See that none of them oxen are bogged down," his father said. John gave no sign that he heard. Rumsey Snelling raised his voice, "You hear what I say?"

"Yeah, Pa, yeah."

Inside the wagon Mrs. Snelling stirred and cleared her throat. A drinking cup rattled. Everyone outside was instantly attentive, staring, listening. Then everything was silent again. The Snellings looked at each other.

Reed said, "I remember when all them folks died at the camp on the Platte. Me and Jeff went around—"

"You shut up," Rumsey said. He raised his head and spat just beyond the toe of his boot. "It ain't fitten to be talking like that before Eddie and his sister." He screwed up his features, staring at the Cushman wagon. "How many was it died in that camp that time?"

Rumsey and Reed fell into an argument about the number. The other Snelling boys listened, their eyes sliding from the debaters to Eddie and Kathy. Eddie wanted to yell at them to shut up. He felt weak.

Like everything they started, the Snellings' argument arrived nowhere. Reed and his father lost track of the original subject and talked of a man who had died of snake bite on the Little Blue.

Suddenly Mrs. Snelling was looking out under the wagon bow. Her face was gaunt, yellowish, shining with sweat. She climbed down slowly. She put both hands against the small of her back as she straightened up, looking at Eddie and Kathy.

"They're dead," Eddie said.

"Yes." Mrs. Snelling brushed at lank graying hair with her forearm. "They went about the same time, I think." She came forward and started to take Kathy in her arms. Kathy clung tighter to her brother.

"You poor babies," Mrs. Snelling said. "Oh, you poor babies!" She stooped and put her arms around them both. There were tears on her face. The odor of her sweat was a terrible sourness.

The Snelling men came from the shade of their wagon like a flock of moulting chickens rising from the dust. Rumsey fumbled with his beard with a big gray-knuckled hand. "The Lord giveth, and He taketh."

Eddie pushed away from Mrs. Snelling's embrace. "Are you sure?" he asked, the question that all men use to try to block final acceptance of death.

"You poor babies," Mrs. Snelling said, and turned away.

"The Lord giveth, and He taketh," Rumsey said again, as if he had not been heard the first time, "and no one can do nothing about it." He scratched his belly with both hands as he walked over to the Cushman children. "You're among friends, Eddie boy. It's a blow, but you and Kathy are with us and you're going to be taken care of."

"We're not with you!" Eddie said. "I know what you mean by taking care of us."

His hot stare made Rumsey look away. "Now ain't that the beatin'est thing," Rumsey said.

Kathy bumped against Eddie as he walked over to the Cushman wagon. It was a frightening thing and he didn't know whether he had the courage for it, but he could take nobody's word for this. "You stay here," he told Kathy, and broke away from her and climbed into the wagon.

When he got out of the wagon there was no doubt left.

"You just take it easy, Eddie," Rumsey said. "Ma and the boys will do everything we got to do." He put his hand on the rear wheel of the wagon and tried to shake it, his eyes roving over the strong, sound spokes.

"Nobody has to take care of us," Eddie said, but he was ashamed of his words immediately, not because of Rumsey but because of Mrs. Snelling. He saw her watching him with a tired expression, a big-framed woman whose flesh had shrunk and dried until it was almost like the folds of her shapeless dress. She had stayed with Eddie's parents day and night during their sickness, doing everything for them she could.

"Sure, sure, Eddie boy," Rumsey said. "We're all together. We'll get along all right. I thought a heap of your folks and now it's like you and Kathy was kids of mine. Ain't that right, Ma?" He turned and looked at his wife.

Mrs. Snelling watched her husband steadily for a moment and some hot, lingering spirit of rebellion came to her expression, and then it faded away under tiredness and resignation. She walked away without answering.

Rumsey shook the wheel again. He looked at the sky, squinting as if he could read facts from it. "We'd better get an early start tomorrow. We can't risk getting caught by snow in the mountains, Eddie." His hand lay on the wheel as if he owned the wagon. "We'll give your folks a decent burial and then we'll have to hop around, making a few switches with the wagons and things."

The Cushman children stared at him. The weakness in Rumsey which had been repulsive to Eddie before was now frightening.

"We ain't switching anything about this wagon," Eddie said. "I can handle it."

"Sure, sure." Rumsey's eyes shifted. "It's just that we got to help each other, like we did before, that's all I mean."

Kathy was still hard against Eddie, like a scared puppy. She hadn't cried a tear. Eddie thought that was brave of her and yet, vaguely, it worried him. She was wide-eyed, stunned, like the time she had wandered in between the two coiled rattlesnakes and had stood there too scared to move when they rattled.

"You go over and see Lizzie for a while," Eddie said.

Kathy shook her head.

"Go on now. I got to help do some things. You go over there and maybe Lizzie will let you hold the baby."

"Sure, now, Kathy, you do that," Rumsey said. "Me and Eddie have got to work out some problems."

Kathy gave Rumsey a quick look and then she pressed in tighter against her brother.

"Women beat all. I swear they do." Rumsey looked irritably at Kathy, as if he wanted to slap her.

If he tries to lay a hand on her I'll get Pa's rifle out of the wagon and kill him, Eddie thought; but an instant later he realized there was no real viciousness in Rumsey, but only the sharp impatience of the shiftless.

Lizzie gave the baby to her mother and came over.

She was a pinch-faced girl, Lizzie Snelling, with an earnest expression. Her eyes were still red from the salt that had blown into them on the desert east of Ruby Valley. Her dress was mainly rags. She wore shapeless boots that one of her brothers had outgrown. She reached a brown, thin hand down to Kathy.

"Come on, Kathy, you and me can go barefooted in the mud again down at the river."

The boys had edged over to the Cushman wagon. Reed and John were trying to peer in. Jefferson, who was fifteen, grinned and said, "If you want to, Lizzie, you can take off your clothes and wash all over, like the time we seen you—"

"I'm tired of that talk!" Rumsey said. He raised his arm threateningly, but Jeff was too far away to reach.

Holding Kathy's hand, Lizzie stooped and picked up a rock. She stepped toward Jeff and he ducked around the wagon. "Stop that goddam fighting," Rumsey whined. "I'm trying to think."

Lizzie led Kathy away. For a while Kathy held back, looking to Eddie. The baby began to cry, nuzzling at Mrs. Snelling's bosom. Since somewhere in Nebraska she'd had no milk to nurse it. She held it in her arms, staring down the Humboldt. She went to the grub box and began to stir around in it.

"We got a lot of things to figure out," Rumsey said. He spat tobacco juice, frowning. He rubbed his hand across his beard, and then he pursed his lips like a sucker fish, trying to assume the air of a man with a multitude of important tasks. "Reed, you and John get the bars. Jeff, you get a pick and—"

"Ain't no bars," Reed said. "Somebody lost 'em."

"Borry Ashley's—I mean Eddie's," Rumsey said. "You won't mind, Eddie boy, will you?"

"We'd better borry their picks and shovels too," John said. "Our pick's all blunted and the shovel's got a busted back."

"I'll sharpen that pick one of these days. Aimed to at Fort Hall, but I had a power of things to do." Rumsey walked out from the Cushman wagon and scraped two X-marks in the stony ground with the side of his boot. "Right here. I'll say when to stop digging."

"That's hard ground, Pa," John protested. "If we was to go down by the river—"

"Right here!" Rumsey shouted. "By God, I'm running things around here!"

The Snelling boys unlashed tools from the Cushman wagon. Rumsey walked back and forth, giving orders. "Listen at him," Reed muttered. "He says dig where the goddam ground is mostly all rock."

Jeff said, "Eddie's got to help us. It's his folks."

"I'm the one to say who works!" Rumsey shouted. "Eddie don't need to help. He's the bereaved." He liked the sound of his last word and so he repeated it.

Eddie felt the need of physical action, of something to take his mind off what had happened. The worst of it all would be when the Snellings finished digging the graves. Maybe it would be best if Kathy didn't see the last of it; but he knew that all along this trail to California children had stood beside shallow holes at some nameless stopping place and watched such scenes; and parents had seen their children go down into endless silence.

He was trying to make a decision that he wasn't old enough to make. He was ready to cry now, but he wouldn't do it before the Snellings, pecking at the ground over there. Rumsey had come back to the shade of the wagon. He remembered more of his authority and said, "John, did you see about the oxen when you was down at the river?"

"I didn't see none bogged down." John pried at a rock with the pick, cursing the stony ground. "Come to think on it, I didn't see the Cushmans' spare oxen down there a-tall." He took the opportunity to rest and think. The other diggers leaned on their tools, watching him. "By Ned, I don't think that team was there last night, either. I aimed to say something about it, but I guess I forgot." He dropped the pick. "I'll go look."

"I'll go." It was Eddie's chance to get away.

As he passed the Snelling wagon Mrs. Snelling said, "It looks like I'm plumb out of fixin's for this young one, Eddie. I wonder . . ." She did not finish and there was a world of shame in her expression. Eddie's mother had said that Mrs. Snelling was really a decent, prideful woman, and that only the good Lord knew why she had married Rumsey.

Mrs. Snelling kept stirring in her empty food box. "I wonder, Eddie, if I could . . ." The baby kept wailing.

"Help yourself," Eddie said. He went toward the river.

The spare team his father had traded for at Fort Hall was gone. Eddie knew it at a glance, but he went on out through the grass and into the river itself, where the oxen could be wallowed down in the mud and water. He walked back and forth, but he knew they were not there. The other team was there and the Snellings' two oxen, cooling their alkali-rotted feet in the mud. Rock, the Cushmans' saddle horse, was there too, limping from a pulled tendon incurred while helping haul the Snelling wagon up a hill.

Eddie took the blame. His job was to watch the oxen. Yesterday and today, when his parents had been so sick, he hadn't been able to think straight and he hadn't checked at all to make sure the animals were all right.

Lizzie and Kathy were wading in the mud, but Eddie did not stop to ask them about the team. He went down-river looking for tracks and then back up the river, and there he found the broad marks of the strayed team, going east. It looked as if they had set in to travel all the way back to the States.

Eddie went back to the wagons. The Snellings hadn't made much progress with the digging. "Ben and Cross are gone."

"Damn you, John," Rumsey grumbled, "why didn't you say something last night when you saw they was gone? Always trouble and hard luck, and you don't make it no easier."

"I forgot," John said sullenly. "There was too much excitement around here, what with Eddie's folks getting

ready to die and all. Them oxen ain't gone far anyway."
He threw the pick down. "I'll take the horse and go look."

"I'll look myself," Eddie said. Oxen, when they made
up their minds to it, could stray plenty far. He wasn't
going to have John or any other Snelling abusing old sore-
legged Rock by trying to gallop him. The Snellings were
just no damn good.

"We'll look in the morning," Rumsey said. "Maybe
they'll show up before then. Of course, it'll throw us behind another day, and with the snow due before long . . .
A man don't know just what to do."

Eddie knew what he was going to do; he was going after
the oxen. The Snellings might get by with one worn-out
team but that wasn't the way Ashley Cushman had done
things. Eddie's father had traded off worn-down oxen for
another pair that had had time to recuperate at Fort Hall
after being left there by previous emigrants; and he had
figured on doing the same thing again at Big Meadows
before striking out for the Truckee and the Sierras.

Eddie started toward the wagon for his father's rifle.
Indians had been the least of the problems all the way from
Independence, but still you didn't go anywhere without a
rifle, not even after strayed oxen. But he stopped before
he climbed into the wagon. Once had been enough; he
didn't want to go in there again, not until after his parents were buried.

"That's better," Rumsey said. "No use to stir around
so late in the day. We'll go after them in the morning."

"I didn't change my mind," Eddie said. "I was going
after the rifle, but I guess I don't need it."

A flash of sympathy touched Rumsey's eyes. He understood, enough to say, "Take my gun there, long's you
got your mind set on traipsing after something that'll
probably wander back tonight."

For an instant Eddie wanted to accept Rumsey's wish-
ful thinking, but he knew that strayed oxen wouldn't come
back again without help; and it gave him a good reason
for being away while his parents were buried. He took
the bridle and Rumsey's old rifle and went down to get
Rock. The rifle was as disreputable as the Snelling wagon,
a converted flintlock with a broken stock that was bound
with rawhide.

The Snellings watched Eddie walk away. One of the
younger boys hauled himself up to peer into the Cush-

man wagon. He dropped back, scared but fascinated by what he had seen. "Their nose holes look funny," he said, and dared his brothers to take a peek.

Rumsey squirmed around until he was comfortably seated in the shade of the Cushman wagon. "God-al-mighty-fried-hooks, you ain't getting nowhere digging! They'll be smelling before you get the job done."

"Ground's fearful hard," Reed said. "Eddie should've helped us. After all, it's his folks that up and died."

Mrs. Snelling heard her husband and sons talking. She looked at the pinched face of her youngest child and thought of the twenty years behind her. But there was no use in that. She looked across the vast, brutal land, down the long trail to California, praying silently that when they reached the new place there would be a change in Rumsey and the boys, that this move would do them some good, for it was costing her more than the weariness within her. It was taking the very last of her self-respect.

She watched Eddie going toward Lizzie and Kathy down at the river. Girl children were a blessing. Already Lizzie was at an age where you could talk to her, confide in her and rest some of the soul-load on her. The Lord should have given her more girls. The boys, from the time they could walk, had each been another Rumsey Snelling, made in his image and rapidly acquiring his ways.

But Lizzie was different, and Mrs. Snelling could sense that the baby would be different too. She batted at a green-winged stinging fly that tried to settle on the infant's face. A fear that she couldn't allow clutched her as she looked at the tiny features. There were still months to go before they reached California.

Shadows in the gaunt, fanged mountains on the left had changed a little. There was a faint haze on the desolate land that stretched away forever. Mrs. Snelling knew how insignificant the two wagons were, how old and uncaring the land was, and how far it was to anywhere.

The boys wrangled about the digging of the graves. Rumsey said irritably, "There'll be some doin's if I have to get up and come over there."

Down at the river Kathy saw the bridle and said quickly, "Where you going, Eddie?"

"After Ben and old Cross. I'll be back pretty soon."

Kathy ran to him. "I'm going with you."

"You stay with Lizzie. I'll be back pretty soon." Eddie went to Rock and put the bridle on. The horse was still limping slightly, but it would be all right for a slow ride, staying close to sod by the river.

"I'm going, too," Kathy said.

"You can't go!"

If his little sister had cried then, Eddie would have known it was only a temper tantrum. He could have turned her over to Lizzie and gone his way. But Kathy didn't cry. Her face was set with determination and she was white and frightened.

"Rock is already lame," Eddie said. "It's bad enough for me to be riding him, without—"

"I'll take care of you, Kathy," Lizzie said. "If Eddie ain't back by dark you can sleep with me." She took the little girl's hand again and for a time it seemed that Kathy had listened to her and was going to make no fuss.

Eddie scrambled up on the horse.

"Here," Lizzie said. From somewhere she had produced two biscuits and now she held them out to the boy, looking straight at him.

They were old, old and hard, Eddie saw at a glance; and yet, something in Lizzie's face said they were precious, that she was giving of herself when she offered them.

"How long have you had those?" he asked.

"Before we ever got to Fort Hall," Lizzie answered, taking the literal meaning of his question. She held the dabs of hard flour in her slim brown hand, watching him steadily.

Some instinct told Eddie it would be a great offense not to take the offering. He reached down and took the biscuits, feeling the rocklike hardness of them as he put them into his shirt pocket. He said, "Thanks."

Lizzie still watched him with a curiously disturbing expression, as if seeking to see whether he made light of her gift, if he fully understood what she had done. Her hand came down to her side slowly and she said, "Don't worry about Kathy."

Eddie rode away. He went twenty feet before Kathy broke away from Lizzie with a scream that was like mortal hurt. She came running after Rock and grabbed Eddie's leg when he stopped the horse. "Don't leave me, Eddie!"

There were depths in human experience that a boy of thirteen had no reason to know or even wonder about, but this day had opened some of them to Eddie Cushman, and if he did not understand completely what he saw, he was striving to understand. He looked inquiringly at Lizzie and she nodded, a thin-faced girl with dead-serious eyes and a knowledge too heavy for her years.

Lizzie helped Kathy onto the horse. Kathy put her arms around her brother and old Rock limped away slowly.

After a time Kathy began to cry and then Eddie was crying too, so that for a while he could not see or did not care about seeing the tracks of the oxen that he was seeking.

When Eddie twisted to look back, Lizzie was going toward the camp. The Snellings were standing idly around the work they had started. The two wagons were very small and the grim mountains beyond them were very large.

CHAPTER TWO

E<small>DDIE</small> did not find his span of oxen that day. Coolness hastened in after the sun went down and with the fading of the light soon afterward there came a quick cold. It was a long way back to the wagons. Eddie wished now he had taken Rumsey's advice about waiting until morning to start the search.

Eddie was closer to the oxen now. Tomorrow he would find them and drive them back. Once he was driving the wagon, moving with a purpose again, he would feel much better.

He and Kathy huddled in a nest of long grass. They had eaten the biscuits, hard and tasteless, and, Eddie suspected, full of dead weevils. Rock stomped around in the higher grass toward the river. Now and then Eddie stood up to peer at him and make sure he was still there, and occasionally he went down to talk to the horse so Rock wouldn't think he was alone here and go wandering back to the wagons.

Kathy asked, "Are there many Indians here?"

"Naw, just Diggers of all kinds."

"What are *they?*"

Eddie didn't know, but he had heard two grizzled old

mountain men talking about them at Fort Hall, and the
two frontiersmen didn't think highly of them.

"What's it like in heaven, Eddie?"

It was a strange question, especially when Eddie was
worrying about Indians. "I don't know," he answered.
"Pretty, I guess, with lots of clear water and everything
all green and warm."

"There's golden streets too. Do people go there as soon
as they die?"

"Right away." Eddie knew what she was thinking. He
wanted to cry again. He said, "I got to look at Rock."

It was colder out under the stars. The horse was standing quietly in the tall grass. Eddie patted its neck and
talked to it and hurried back to Kathy.

They went to sleep with Rumsey's old rifle beside them,
capped and charged. Kathy was restless, flailing her hands,
twisting. Later on she settled down, holding tightly to Eddie, so that once when he tried to rise to go look at Rock,
he had to struggle to disengage her hands. Still asleep,
she murmured, "Don't leave me alone."

It seemed colder at dawn. Rock was standing a few
rods from where he had been at dark, his breath showing
in the pale light.

"We'll find the oxen pretty soon," Eddie said. "Then
we'll go back to the wagons." Kathy's face was pale and
drawn, with blue smudges under her eyes. "I wish you'd
stayed with Lizzie."

They went on up the river. Before dark the night before, Eddie had lost the tracks but he was sure the oxen
would be somewhere near the water. After a while he
recognized a hill where the road turned away completely
from the Humboldt. As he remembered, it had taken three
or four days to get the wagons through the hills to where
the trail touched the river again. Even if he found the oxen
in the next few minutes, he doubted that he could drive
them back to the wagons before dark.

"I don't feel very good," Kathy said.

"You're hungry. So am I. We'll go a little ways farther
and then if we don't find them, we'll go back and the
Snellings will have to come and help us."

"They won't help."

Leaving the general course of the trail made Eddie uneasy. The trail, no matter if it was only two distant ruts
sighted on a hill, or the glimpse of a piece of broken wag-

on, or abandoned furniture beside an old camp site, was something that spoke of fellow human beings, of a home that he and Kathy had once known, and of a home they were to know at the end of the trip.

The farther he rode from the bleak hill where the trail turned from the river, the more worried he became. One hill was like another. One turn of the river had the sameness of the last turn, and although he thought he could always follow the river back to the wagons, Eddie's fear of getting lost was growing. He was just about scared enough to go back without the oxen when he saw them grazing in a little swale ahead.

Finding them was a tremendous relief and a great accomplishment. "There they are! What did I tell you, Kathy? There they are!" The oxen eyed the horse complacently, twitching their loose hides against flies. Eddie called out their names. He turned to share his elation with Kathy.

She was pale. She was not interested in Cross and Ben. She slid down from the horse suddenly and began to vomit. Eddie scrambled down and steadied her head. "It's the heat," he said, "the doggone sun and going without anything to eat and all." Kathy shuddered and retched.

"We'll make it back to the wagons tonight, Kathy. Mrs. Snelling can fix you something to eat and then you'll be all right."

"I don't want anything to eat."

Eddie took his sister to the river and helped her wash her face. She drank some water and said she felt better. It was a chore getting her back on old Rock and then getting on himself, with the awkward rifle in the way. At last he leaned the rifle against the side of the horse and dragged it up barrel first after he was mounted.

He turned the oxen down the river and they went willingly enough, their bellies rumbling as they swayed along.

"You feeling better now, Kathy?"

Kathy didn't have time to slide off the horse. She could only turn her head as the water she had just drunk came gushing out, and then the retching started again. Eddie helped her down and let her lie in the warm grass. "It was those biscuits," he said. "Lizzie carried them around so long, there's no telling what was in them."

The oxen turned and started up the river again. Eddie had to run to head them off. When he got back to Kathy she was sitting up. He got on Rock first this time but when he tried to haul Kathy up behind him she was too weak to help herself, so he had to get down and boost her up and then go through the awkward process of scrambling up with the heavy rifle. He wished he'd put the saddle on.

During the time it took to get Kathy and himself mounted the oxen turned up-river again. Eddie got them started in the right direction once more and they all went a quarter of a mile without trouble. Then Kathy was sick again and had to get down.

Eddie was scared cold. He tried to remember how far it was to the wagons, or even how far it was to where the trail came close to the river after crossing the hills. Maybe there was another train working through the hills now, a big outfit like the one his folks had travelled with to Fort Hall, run by competent men, with a lot of women who knew all about the ailments of little girls like Kathy.

"You ride and hold onto Rock's mane and I'll lead him. Can you do that, Kathy?"

Kathy nodded.

Again Eddie had to turn the oxen from their hard-headed desire to go up-river. He got them going again, leading the horse, carrying the heavy rifle, looking back frequently at the pale, sick little figure on the horse. Progress was agonizing. The intervals between Kathy's cramps and the retching that almost tore her apart grew shorter. Each time she couldn't stay on the horse.

It was late afternoon when they came to the trail. The hot sun lay in a long swath on the brown hills, rutted where wagons had made the steep descent; but there were no wagons in sight now and when Eddie went over and looked hopefully at the trail he saw wheel marks blown full of sand, as if no one had passed for years.

"It ain't so far now, Kathy." Eddie looked at the sun and knew they had no chance to get back to the camp before dark, but they had to keep going; he had to get Kathy to Mrs. Snelling as soon as he could.

He abandoned the oxen. They were no longer important. Some bovine perverseness in the animals threw a circuit in their brains and they now followed the horse.

Before sundown Kathy was too weak to stay on Rock by herself. Eddie left the rifle beside the trail, propping it upright with rocks so that one of the Snellings would have no trouble finding it tomorrow. He got Kathy to stay on the horse long enough for him to mount behind her. He held her on and rode and now there was no time to stop when the cramps made her cry out or when her efforts to vomit made her small body shudder.

Rock limped down the trail. The oxen lumbered along on the easier footing beside the river. Eddie's arms ached with the strain of holding Kathy and the uneven movement of the horse made his task more difficult.

At dusk Kathy was a weight without strength of her own. She moaned and called for her mother. Sometimes, as if she had just roused from sleep, Kathy asked in a normal voice, "How far is it now?" And Eddie always answered, "Not far. We'll be there soon."

He no longer had faith that everything would change when he reached the wagons. Kathy was sick the same way Eddie's parents had been sick, and they had died in two and a half days in spite of everything that Mrs. Snelling could do.

No, there would be no miracle achieved simply by reaching the camp; but there was still the hope that Kathy's sickness was different in some way, that it wasn't as bad as the cholera could be. A steady hope burned in Eddie, an argument against Kathy's dying that he tried to base to bits of logic that he gathered from everything he had heard about the sickness.

But he held no longer a blind, unthinking faith in the powers or wisdom of adults. His parents, who had been an unquestioned source of strength and discipline, were gone; and the other grown-ups he must depend on in this crisis lacked his trust. Still, they were the only source of help.

In the dark his arms grew so tired as Kathy sagged against him that he had to stop and get down. He fell to the ground with his sister on top of him, lacking for a time the strength to use his arms. The horse stood like its name, shifting weight from its sore leg, blowing dust from its nostrils.

Kathy murmured plaintively, "Are we there?"

"Pretty soon now. It's not far. Lizzie and Mrs. Snelling will take care of you."

After a while Eddie lifted Kathy in his arms. He tried to lay her across the horse so that he could mount, but when he let go of her and tried to get up, she slid to the ground and cried out sharply, "Don't leave me!"

He tied the reins together and put them around his

arm. He lifted Kathy again and stumbled down to the creek with her and there he put her down, floundering about in the darkness until he found a bank high enough to mount from, while Rock stood in the creek. Holding the dead weight of Kathy in his arms, he got on the horse and went on.

Soon again he was tired, with his shoulder sockets burning. Again and again as the night wore on Eddie had to get down to rest and then to seek another place in the creek where Rock's back would be low enough so that he could get on with Kathy in his arms.

His eyes strained to see a campfire. The Snellings would have a big one, and for all their traveling with people who followed the rules, they wouldn't bother to put out their fire when they went to bed. But there was only velvety darkness around Eddie and the feeling of great space on all sides.

Some time during the night he led the horse into a place where the mud was deep and yielding. When Eddie tried to ride out of the river the mud held tight against Rock's legs and the horse stumbled trying to get up the bank, pitching Eddie and Kathy into the stream. That was when Rock hurt his injured leg again so that he could barely hobble.

Eddie removed the bridle and tied it around Rock's neck so that it wouldn't be lost when he came back to get the horse, and so the reins wouldn't drag and trip old Rock. He took his sister in his arms and walked, searching the night for the glow of a fire. The grass caught at his legs and bumps and hummocks made him stumble. He was afraid to cut back to the trail, somewhere on his left, because he knew he might miss it and cross it and go wandering toward the mountains.

Kathy's body was burning hot against him, her bowels had run, and the wretched cramping still racked her. He gave her water from his hands whenever she wanted it, but it seemed to make the cramping worse.

It was a night that Eddie never remembered clearly afterward; but he did recall when the slow spreading of light began on the mountains. Kathy clung to him and called out for her mother then, and even looked around to see her mother and cried because she was not there.

At dawn Eddie went out on the trail, staggering through

the dust that he kicked up in the cold air. When full light came he saw the wagons far ahead. He shouted and tried to run toward them but the effort made him stumble and gasp with weariness. He went another full mile before the wagons grew any larger in his vision.

The Snellings weren't up yet. He could see no smoke. They ought to get up. They would see him then, out here on the trail, trying to reach them.

After another quarter of a mile Eddie recognized the terrible, stunning wrongness of what he saw.

There was only one wagon.

The full impact hit him when he reached it. While he was struggling toward it he had been thinking that he would have to go back after the oxen that had stopped when he left Rock, and then go on and overtake the Snellings.

But it was the Snelling wagon that was left. All the oxen were gone. The camp was a litter of discarded junk, ragged blankets, battered cooking utensils—all the things the Snellings had discarded when they took over the Cushman wagon.

On the salt desert, Ashley Cushman had loaned Rumsey his spare wheel. That was gone too. The Snelling wagon was resting on an oak bureau that had belonged to Mrs. Cushman.

Eddie put Kathy down on one of the ragged blankets. He stumbled around through scattered harness, past an ill-made yoke stained with blood from the sores it had worn on the necks of Rumsey's oxen. For a few moments he had thought that someone must have been left to tell him and Kathy what to do. There was no one. There was no message. The worthless wagon was propped up on his mother's bureau.

Kathy stirred and saw the wagon for the first time. "Where's Lizzie, Eddie?"

Eddie was not old enough to lie and pretend any longer.

"They're gone. They've gone on and they took our wagon."

He watched Kathy's face and despair gripped him when he gauged the seriousness of her condition by the fact that she was not alarmed by his words. "I want a drink, Eddie."

Eddie picked up an iron pot and started toward the

river. He walked across the place where the Snellings had been digging when he left to find the oxen. They had gone down scarcely three inches. A bitter anger that almost overcame him made him physically ill as he walked on. It would be like the Snellings, too lazy to dig, to drag his parents away from the camp and leave them for the coyotes.

He took water back to Kathy and tried to make her comfortable in the shade. He carried still more water and washed her burning body with it. She seemed to feel better then. Oddly, his mother's clothing and small personal possessions, carried in a small chest, had not been disturbed, and with them, although he didn't think they had been stored there before, were Kathy's dresses. Eddie threw away the filthy dress his sister had worn during the night and put clean clothes on her.

He sat beside her, sponging her face with water, refusing to let the tremendous silence bear upon him, refusing to look at the country around him. All night he stayed beside her. Sometimes her voice came to him from far away, rousing him after he had let his head fall forward on his knees in sleep.

Responsibility was a barb that kept ripping into his exhaustion. It aroused him at times when he had fallen on his side and gone to sleep, even though Kathy was not calling to him. There was no fire and he had lacked time to seek a way of making one.

Lack of facts about the fire site were to become a sore spot later, like nettles wiping across his mind whenever he thought of the subject. He didn't know whether or not there had been warm ashes when he reached the camp, which would have proved that the Snellings had waited two days, at least. But Eddie hadn't investigated the fire site until it was too late to tell how old the ashes were.

Sometime near dawn Kathy died. She had been talking to him lucidly minutes before, talking about Grandma Duncan's orchard in Illinois. She lapsed into silence and Eddie fell asleep for a time. When he jerked back to consciousness—it could not have been very long, he knew —Kathy was dead.

He started to put her into the wagon, but a hatred of the Snellings rose in him so great that even their wagon was an evil thing. He covered Kathy with one of his mother's dresses.

He was too numb then to feel grief. The Snellings had robbed him even of that. Eddie fell asleep wondering why he couldn't cry. The hot sun woke him up hours later. Even though his mind tried to snap back quickly to his troubles, there was some vagueness now interposed between the facts around him and his reaction to them.

A stolid sort of daze was on him. He broke out of it only once during the morning, sobbing without tears because of the way the broken-backed shovel the Snellings had left behind kept buckling when he tried to dig into the sod near the river. Both Eddie and shovel were too weak for the job.

He had to dig Kathy's grave at the very edge of the water.

On his way back to the wagon he discovered the graves of his parents. At least the Snellings had buried them. He knew there should be rocks heaped upon the graves, but when he cast around he could find only small stones. After a time the sheer futility of the task stopped him.

He went back to camp and looked for food.

Trampled in the dust were some kernels of corn and a handful of grain from the store Ashley Cushman had saved to give his oxen on the last hard haul across the Sierras. Eddie plucked what he could from the dirt and sat chewing, staring into space.

He wasn't going to California. It was an accursed dream, and everything that had happened here at Gravelly Crossing could be laid to it. Eddie was going back to Grandfather Duncan and the orchards Kathy had talked of last night.

Although his remembrance of Grandfather Duncan, his home, his fields and barns was vague, still they were things known; they were real. What lay somewhere else was only a misty dream that killed. Eddie chewed the hard grain and the gritty corn. The trail back home didn't seem so bad, so long. He would take a blanket. He would find the rifle where he had left it, and he would go home.

He searched through the camp thoroughly. The Snellings had taken everything edible or useful except the things in his mother's little chest, and they were of no use to Eddie Cushman. All he carried away was a ragged gray blanket as he went up the river. For the next ten days his life reverted to the fulfilling of two savage needs, hunger and shelter.

He found the rifle and the shot and powder where he had left it. Of Rock he never saw any sign again, but he came upon the two oxen when his hunger had long passed the gnawing, growling stage. Eddie knelt and aimed at Ben.

The cap had been on the nipple for days and it was dampened by dew and frost. It did not explode. Ben kept staring moodily at Eddie. With a fresh cap, Eddie aimed again and then he lowered the rifle. He had no knife and the hide of an ox was too tough to tear with the hands.

He went without food that day. The next evening he caught mice as they rustled in the grass. He ripped the skins off with his hands and gutted them with his forefinger. He gagged the first time he ate them. The following day he found a dead gull. He had cramps soon after he ate it.

Eddie never had clear remembrance of his journey up the Humboldt and on to Ruby Valley.

It must have been about the tenth day when he saw the trading post. A wagon train was just leaving it. Eddie could think of nothing he wanted from an emigrant train. There might be people in it who would feel obliged to take him with them to California.

He waited until the wagons were far away before he went toward the post. Two big gray dogs charged out. They walked around him, bristling, stiff-legged. He paid no attention to them as he went on, and the dogs, puzzled by his attitude, fell in behind him, sniffing at the sun-blackened remains of the jack rabbit he had been carrying and eating on for two days.

A woman came from the house, shading her eyes with her hand. She called and a man came out to stand beside her. The woman walked forward. "I swear those dogs are acting strange, as if they know him."

She kept staring at the approaching figure, who wore a shirt made of a blanket scrap with a head hole and a strip of cloth tied around the middle. The dogs sniffed at the rabbit. They jumped away and wagged their tails apologetically when Eddie stumbled and made a quick motion to recover balance.

The woman cried, "My God, Hildreth, it's a white boy!"

The man was big, taller than Eddie's father, with piercing eyes under heavy, dark brows. "Where'd you come from, son?" he asked in a deep, puzzled tone.

"From Illinois." Eddie's voice was strange to him.

"That's a fair piece." The man glanced at his wife and then he turned his shrewd, penetrating look on Eddie again. There was kindness and understanding in his expression. He seemed to sense that a grim tale lay behind Eddie's sudden appearance here. He studied Eddie's worn boots, his ragged clothes, and the thin, starved look of him. "Are you hungry?"

"I guess so." It was hard for Eddie to think of food other than that which you shot at close range or caught with your hands.

"From Illinois?" The woman looked at her husband with a puzzled expression. "Where's your folks?"

"Dead," Eddie said.

"On the trail?"

Eddie nodded.

Mrs. Hildreth thought she was getting the story straightened out. There was some of the gaunt tiredness of Mrs. Snelling in her expression, but she wasn't like Mrs. Snelling at all, Eddie knew. She was strong and competent looking, the kind of woman who might have been able to save his parents if they had taken sick here instead of out there on the river.

"You poor thing!" A power of sympathy came into Mrs. Hildreth's face. She reached out and put her hand on Eddie's shoulder. He jerked away from her touch, startling one of the dogs that had lain down behind him.

"Leave him alone, Bess," Hildreth said. "You want to wash up and have something to eat, son?"

"Thanks." Eddie's voice sounded strange to him, and the voices of the Hildreths were strange after his days of listening to the gulls. He felt that he could not spare many words, and at the same time he wanted to let his whole story out with a rush.

Mrs. Hildreth said, "But where are the rest of your wagons? The train that just left here hadn't passed anybody on the trail. If you were coming—"

"Never mind," Hildreth said. "Come on, son. What's your name?"

"Eddie."

"I see." Hildreth didn't ask about a last name. He led the boy down to a creek and filled a cut-down barrel with water. "Take off your clothes and wallow, Eddie."

Two squaws were cooking at a fire under a pole-and-bough shade that ran out from the end of one of the buildings. They glanced with curiosity at the scene. Ordinarily, Eddie would have been greatly embarrassed by their presence, but now he paid no attention to them as he undressed and stepped into the tub. Hildreth gave him a handful of soft soap from a wooden keg.

"Did you run into much game?" Hildreth asked.

Eddie watched the gray run off his body as he scrubbed away with his hands in the tepid water. He shook his head. Hildreth was shaking the dust from his clothes. "I'll see if Ma can't rustle up something for you to wear after you've had a bite to eat."

When Eddie was dressing Hildreth held out the scrap of blanket. Eddie looked at it and his lips grew thin. He hurled it away. But he took the rifle that had belonged to Rumsey Snelling when he went to the house with Hildreth.

Sitting in a chair at a table gave Eddie a strange sensation. He picked up a fork and stared at the food on his plate and then he began to eat and each bite brought on a ravenous desire for more.

"It's best to take it a little easy, if you haven't had too much to eat lately," Hildreth said. "How long you been out by yourself?"

"A long time," Eddie said. He realized how intently the Hildreths were watching him and it made him uneasy.

Mrs. Hildreth said, "If that train this morning didn't pass anyone on the salt desert, you must have come from somewhere down the Humboldt. Didn't you?"

"Let him eat," Hildreth said.

Eddie put his fork down. He had come from Gravelly Crossing, and he wished he could forget it. His feeling that it should not be talked about was hardening.

"A couple, three weeks ago there was two wagons here, one with a passel of boys," Mrs. Hildreth said. "Are you one of them?"

"No!" The sight of his food was revolting to Eddie. Already, what he had eaten was tormenting his stomach. He wasn't one of the dirty, lousy Snellings, and he wished the woman would stop talking.

"The other wagon—the good one—had a boy—" The woman's eyes narrowed as she glanced from Eddie to her husband—"and that beautiful little girl with golden hair."

"She's dead!" Eddie said. Suddenly he was violently sick. He got up and rushed out of the house.

"Damn it, Bess," Hildreth said, "I told you to leave him alone!"

"I was only trying to find out—"

"I know, I know." Hildreth went out to where Eddie was standing at the end of a building. The two dogs were there in the shade near him. "Never saw old Jug and Pistol take to anyone as easy as they have to you, Eddie. I've trained them not to cotton up to people so as not to have them go off with one of these trains. They sure as hell don't like Indians, you can bet on that."

Hildreth went on talking, about the Indians that came to the post, about their legends of demon birds and fish far back in the mountains. It was obvious to Eddie what the man was trying to do, but still his slow, easy speech began to veer Eddie's mind from its frozen channel.

After a time Hildreth said he had to go to the corral to see about a newborn colt and wondered if Eddie wanted to see it. They walked along together. The dogs sniffed at Eddie's legs in a friendly manner but Hildreth said not to pet them.

In the same easy conversational tone Hildreth asked, "It wasn't Indians, was it?"

"No."

"Sickness?"

Eddie nodded.

"I had to know, you understand, because a train just left here. If it was Indians, we'd have to warn them. That would be the right thing to do, wouldn't it?"

"Sure."

They looked at the newborn colt, all legs and shakiness and ears. Hildreth asked no more questions about Eddie's experience and Eddie stayed away from the house the rest of the day. He helped Hildreth milk two cows that evening. They drank some of the warm milk from the buckets and the foam left a long white streak on Hildreth's great brown beard. Eddie wanted to laugh at the sight but something inside him held him silent.

"Bess won't pester you any more with questions, Eddie. It was just a woman's way, wanting to know what happened so she could give you sympathy."

"I don't need any."

"Sure," Hildreth said softly, but he looked troubled.

Eddie slept that night on a feather mattress in the warm shelter of the house. When he went to sleep he drifted away with a feeling of security, hearing the low voices of the Hildreths in the kitchen. But in the night he had bad dreams. The demon bird of Indian legend that Hildreth had mentioned so briefly was swooping down to tear Kathy from Eddie's arms as he stumbled through the night toward a campfire where his parents waited.

Sometimes he had a gun and he tried to shoot the great, white-winged bird as it came striking, but the trigger would never pull, although he strained and pressed and cried out. He woke up sweating and threshing, with Hildreth standing over him, and behind the big figure, Mrs. Hildreth with a candle.

"You're all right, Eddie. You're all right now," Hildreth said. "You're not out in the night any more."

Mrs. Hildreth straightened the covers. She was careful not to touch Eddie and her talk was gruff and matter-of-fact as she moved about the bed; but when she picked up the candle again and turned to go away with her husband, Eddie saw tears on her cheeks.

The Hildreths sat in the kitchen until Eddie went to sleep again. He slept soundly the rest of the night, but when he woke up the dream still bothered him.

CHAPTER THREE

Eddie had been in Ruby Valley a week when an Army captain rode in with part of a troop of cavalry on their way to the Mormon settlements east of the salt desert. The captain was a graying, hard-shaved man, as brown as coffee under the layers of dust on him.

"We'll stay overnight with you and drink up some of your good water, Sam, if you don't mind," the captain said to Hildreth. "What's been going on?"

"Same old thing," Hildreth said. He put his hand on Eddie's shoulder. "Trains are starting to peter out for the summer. The Indians will be drifting in to get their usual robbing before long."

The captain grinned. "Robbing, indeed." He put a

sharp look on Eddie. "Where'd you get the new helper?"

"His uncle dropped him off here last week. They weren't getting along and Eddie thought he'd like to stay."

Eddie learned the value of a casual lie. The captain looked him over, said, "So?" and forgot about him. "There's a burned wagon at Gravelly Crossing, Sam."

Hildreth glanced toward the kitchen doorway, where his wife was listening. "It was abandoned, Walworth. Some Shoshones burned it."

"How do you know?"

"A couple of Wahno's bucks went past here a few days ago. They told me."

Captain Walworth worked dust from his lips and spat. He nodded without interest. "We noticed one wheel seemed to be missing. We found three people, a man, a woman and a little girl. They'd been buried but the coyotes had dragged them out." He slapped dust from his thigh and shook his head. "These damned emigrants will keep coming, with no idea of what they're up against."

Eddie was filled with an inarticulate rage. He felt Hildreth's grip tightening on his shoulder, but he wanted to break free and strike the captain, to smash him down and make him understand that he didn't know what he was talking about.

"You buried them again, of course?" Hildreth said.

"We did what we could. What can you do without wasting half a day?" Walworth brushed at his sleeves. "Have you got a drink of that decent whisky left, Sam, or are you going to keep me here in the sun the rest of the day?"

"There's some left." Hildreth gave Eddie a little push. "See if the red cow is trying to shove down the corral fence again, will you, Eddie?"

The captain and Hildreth went toward the house as Eddie walked away. He looked at the cavalrymen preparing to camp near the creek. His anger at the captain's curt dismissal of what he had seen at Gravelly Crossing settled away to a bleakness, leaving the hard knowledge that nobody much gave a damn what happened to an individual in this world. You took care of yourself, like the miserable Snelling tribe.

But Eddie resolved that he wouldn't be like the Snellings. He would be hard and strong, asking nothing from anyone, giving nothing either, taking care of himself.

That night he wouldn't sleep in the house because Captain Walworth was there, his dark face showing a tint of red from Hildreth's whisky. Eddie went to the barn. Mrs. Hildreth fretted about it and didn't understand, but her husband did. He came out and said, "These army people get pretty hard, seeing everything they do along this part of the trail, Eddie. If Walworth had known who you were—"

"Why'd you lie to him?"

"I thought that's what you wanted. He would have questioned the very devil out of you. I knew you didn't want that, did you?"

"No."

"That's why I lied to him. There wasn't anything he could do but ask questions. If you don't want to stay here, I can tell him the truth. He can take you as far east as the Mormon settlements and then maybe he can arrange to have soldiers going on to the States take you back with them. I think you know you're welcome to stay here but I won't beg you."

"I'll stay. I've got to do something."

Hildreth was quiet for several moments. "Something about the people in the other wagon, Eddie?"

"No. I hope they all die in the mountains."

Eddie could hear Hildreth's slow breathing in the gloomy barn, and then Hildreth said, "Do you want to tell me about what happened?"

"No." The whole story was getting entangled deeper in Eddie's determination not to talk about it. When he first came into the yard, when he saw the strength and kindness in Hildreth's eyes, he had been on the verge of blurting it all out; and then Mrs. Hildreth's sympathy had become too strong; she had touched him, and driven his feelings back in upon themselves.

"You suit yourself," Hildreth said. He paused. "I guess I know what the something is you have to do. Don't you worry about it. I'll take care of it."

Jug and Pistol padded to the door when Hildreth left. They watched him walk back to the house and then they came over and lay down beside Eddie. When he woke in the early morning there was a blanket over him. The cavalrymen were up before dawn. Eddie heard them yawning and cursing as they complained about their way of life. From the doorway of the barn he watched them ride away.

There was another rider already far ahead of them, a man with a pack horse. At first Eddie thought it must be a scout for the soldiers, but the man went toward the down flow of the Humboldt and the cavalrymen went eastward in the hazy light. Then Eddie knew who the lone rider was and where he was going.

At breakfast Mrs. Hildreth asked Eddie if he thought there was any way the corral could be fixed to keep the red cow from causing trouble. Eddie had heard Hildreth talking about it and knew what had to be done. He said, "I think so." He worked hard and steadily during the several days Hildreth was gone, digging holes and setting posts that Hildreth had lacked time to put in place.

When Hildreth came riding back, his brown beard drenched with gray dust, with the pack horse carrying a pick and shovel and heavy bar, he looked at the work Eddie had done and nodded. "We've both done a good job in the last few days, boy."

Eddie wanted to ask questions but he couldn't bring himself to it. He began to unload the pack horse.

"I used rocks and the iron from the wagon," Hildreth said. "The place is well marked, in case you ever go past there."

"Thanks." Eddie felt tears on his cheeks. He kept his face away from Hildreth.

Hildreth began to unsaddle. "That wasn't your wagon. I could tell that much from the condition of the tires. It was the no-good one that was here with you."

"Yeah."

Hildreth said no more while they were taking care of the horses. When he spoke again, in a soft voice, Eddie recognized the deep anger of a quiet man. "Was it your choice not to go with them, or did they— Was there some other reason?"

Eddie did not answer.

"I want to know!" It was the only straight, hard demand Hildreth ever made of Eddie. Eddie knew he had to answer.

"I went after two oxen that ran away. I was gone two days and nights. That's when they left." Eddie didn't want to talk about Kathy, to relive with words the experience of those two days and nights.

The anger began to leave Hildreth. "That's a little different then, but not much." He thought about it and the nature of a reasonable, even-tempered man asserted itself. "It was a worthless outfit, if ever I saw one, to begin with. After two nights they must have thought the Paiutes had got you and they were probably too scared to go look for you. That must have been it. They figured something bad had happened to you and so they just shifted wagons and lit out. You've got to overlook a lot in people like that, Eddie."

There was too much to overlook. It might not have been two nights that the Snellings had waited. They might have left the morning after Kathy and Eddie went away to look for the oxen. Hildreth could make excuses for the Snellings but Eddie couldn't justify their running away, not even on the grounds of utter worthlessness.

"The thing to do," Hildreth said, "is to forget all about them and look ahead."

"Yeah."

"Before long old Sko-kup will be visiting us with his tribe. Now that's a sight to see. You'll have to keep an eye on Pistol and Jug or those Indians will eat them right on our doorsteps." Hildreth slapped Eddie lightly on the shoulder. "Speaking of eating, Bess promised me a dried apple pie when I left the other day. Let's go up to the house and see if she's as good as her word."

"Fine," Eddie said, but as he walked along with Hildreth he was thinking of the Snellings. There was too much that Hildreth didn't know, of Eddie stumbling into the dead camp with Kathy in his arms, of his waiting through the night; and Hildreth didn't know about the broken-backed shovel that had wobbled and slipped and refused to cut the tough sod.

Eddie Cushman stayed three years with the Hildreths in Ruby Valley. He came to know Sko-kup and the Indians of the valley, a bedraggled looking lot who suffered by comparison with the Sioux Eddie had seen on the Great Plains. He came to understand that Indians were merely men of a darker color than his own. Their ways were strange but they were not to be despised because of that. What impressed Eddie most of all about them was their unquestioning acceptance of their own way of life, their lack of bitterness toward the tough, inhospitable land of their birth.

The winters were cold months of cloudless skies when

travelers on the trail were few. Isolation might have overcome some white men, but Hildreth was a man of energy and curiosity. Eddie rode with him when they explored the mountains. They saw the ghostly rising of dawns from high camps. They visited the Indians.

Eddie learned to handle a rifle and a pistol. Hildreth was an expert with both, although he had no great interest in firearms. Before he took the westward trails Hildreth had been a blacksmith. He was a good one. Slowly and with great care he taught Eddie the trade, holding back none of his own special twists. In three years Eddie could not become a master of the trade but he learned well, and after that it would be a matter of experience.

Most of all Eddie took satisfaction in the welding of hot metal. He practiced with old wagon tires, hammering the glowing iron together with quick strokes, gauging the heat by the color, sensing when it was no longer right to strike, and at last he achieved the skill to make a fusion that was strong, with no well defined line of joining.

Work brought a general dulling of his memories of Gravelly Crossing, but still there were times when he remembered sharply and bitterly. Sometimes the iron that he hammered made him recall the use to which Hildreth had put the iron from the burned Snelling wagon, and then the whole remembrance came back so strongly that he would leave the shop and turn to something else.

In the summers the wagon trains came through. Sometimes they had guides, mainly hard-bitten older men who seemed to hold themselves apart from the emigrants. One of the guides, a stringy old man with far-seeing eyes and a general air of bitterness, spent his time in the blacksmith shop where Eddie was helping Hildreth cut down tires for shrunken wagon wheels.

"You've got a good boy there, Hildreth."

Eddie hoisted a cut tire from the forge with a rope that ran through a pulley on the blackened ridge log high overhead, easing off as Hildreth swung the tire so that the ends to be welded came down on the anvil without a second wasted from the fire. "Yep!" Hildreth said between hammer blows.

"Kids don't want to work any more," the guide said. "Everybody wants to go to California and get rich. With all the crooked work going on out there, it ain't no place for an honest man."

"Yep!" Hildreth said.

"Wagon travel is slowing down, thank God, but now they're talking of building a railroad clean through." The guide spat with contempt. "Ain't no steam cars ever going to run over the Sierras, no matter what Johnny Fremont or nobody else says."

Hildreth finished welding the tire and squinted at it critically. Soot from the forge hung in his brown beard. "You may be right, mister," he said.

The States seemed far away to Eddie now. Sheer distance had washed away memories that would have been kept alive if his family had lived. No longer had he any wish to go back to his grandparents in Illinois. He did have a feeling of guilt that he had not tried to send a message back to Grandpa Duncan, telling him what had happened. But Grandpa Duncan had been very old when Eddie last saw him. It might be best for him to go on believing that his daughter and grandchildren had reached California.

If Eddie's memories of the States were dulling, those of the emigrants were not. They talked more of where they had come from than of where they were going, and they carried the troubles of the nation with them. They argued about slavery and the Compromise as if slavery existed out here; and once Eddie saw two bullwhackers freighting with an emigrant train tear bloody gashes in each other in a whip fight caused by a North-South argument.

Rumsey Snelling, Eddie remembered, had been a proslaver, orating loudly about the superiority of white people whenever anyone would listen to him. Maybe he was still shooting off his mouth out in California. Because of him Eddie had long ago taken the other side of the issue without knowing anything about either side.

There was no one like the Snellings in any of the wagons Eddie saw during his summer in Ruby Valley.

The people were all tired when they reached the trading post, and some of their oxen were fit only for shooting; but after a few days of rest there was a remarkable change. As soon as they knew they were going to stay a while, the women prettied up and exposed small luxuries they had hidden from their husbands. The men recovered a willingness to dance and from the big Conestogas they sometimes produced their supplies of finer wines and whisky.

Mixed with a partly hidden fear of the rest of the long haul down the Humboldt, the Forty Mile, and the Sierras, was a gabble of things back home, of politics, of gossip.

Sometimes Eddie felt himself warming toward the emigrants, but each time a dull bitterness came between him and them, for in some way their restlessness and urge to risk their lives were responsible for the tragedy at Gravelly Crossing.

A slender, green-eyed girl in one train became interested in him and seemed to appear wherever he was doing his chores. Her name was Beth Clendenin, and Eddie was to remember her name and her face although he saw her only during three days.

Beth was his own age. One afternoon when he was repairing a broken clevis she stood in the doorway of the shop watching with admiration.

"There's something beautiful in the way you use your hands, Eddie."

Eddie felt the heat rising in his neck and face. He hoped Beth would think it was from the forge.

"Do you like it way out here where there's nothing to see or do?" she asked.

"Sure." Eddie stiffened, feeling a need to defend the Hildreths and himself for being where they were, although he knew that a restlessness and curiosity to see a greater part of the world had developed in him during the summer; perhaps, he thought, an infection from the emigrants. This girl who looked so cool and self-possessed embodied a life that he had missed because illness and cowardice had combined to leave him a frightened boy alone at Gravelly Crossing.

She drove the sense of aloneness deeper into him. "But this land is so wild and useless. You could grow up and be like a hill-billy that doesn't know anything beyond a few miles from home."

"You people are darned glad to stop here."

"Of course. We're glad to find any place where there's water and grass and a chance to rest and pretend to be human beings."

"You mean no one is a human being if he lives here?" Eddie asked angrily.

"No, I don't mean that. It's just that—" Beth couldn't explain it against the anger she saw on Eddie's face. "Of course, you were born here, so I guess that makes a difference."

"Yes, I was born here! Now go on and let me work!"

He was sorry when Beth walked away. He didn't understand his own anger. He tonged the clevis into the slack tub and then dumped it on the dirt floor and stood looking at his hands, big by inheritance, growing broad and powerful from work. There was nothing wrong with the girl's asking questions.

Tomorrow the train was leaving, so tonight he would try to make up with Beth at the dance between the big fires. Maybe if she knew the circumstances that had brought him to Ruby Valley she wouldn't think he was such a clod. He became nervous at the thought of dancing with Beth, although he had danced with other girls from other trains.

That evening when the fiddler was tuning up and the caller was exercising his voice and the Hildreths, who never missed a chance to join in the fun, had already gone to the big fires, Eddie got into Hildreth's whisky to brace his courage. He didn't know how much to take from the jug so he took more than enough.

When he walked down to where the dancers were making great shadows in the firelight, his walk was steady and his face was solemn, but he was joyously drunk inside. He saw Beth dancing with a young man from one of the Kentucky wagons. She didn't look at Eddie. He decided that she was pretending not to notice him.

The dance ended and he walked over to her, feeling a warm glow all through his body. He made a little bow and spoke words he had heard his father use, "May I have the honor of the next dance with you, Miss Clendenin?"

The moving light of the fire showed surprise and pleasure on Beth's face. Her partner stared at Eddie. He was three or four years older than Eddie, tall and dark, with beard just beginning to show strongly on his chin.

Beth said, "Not the next dance, Eddie, but after a while—"

"You're drunk," the Kentuckian said, sniffing and bending to peer into Eddie's eyes. "You ain't dancing with Beth. Go on back to the blacksmith shop, kid."

It was not the name, or the charge of drunkenness, or even the older man's arrogant superiority that enraged Eddie Cushman, but rather that he seemed to be making fun of the words Eddie had spoken, that he was attacking the memory of Eddie's parents.

Eddie thought no farther than that. He made no threats along conventional lines. He said nothing; he merely hit the tall Kentuckian as hard as he could. He had to reach and to lift the swing to make it carry.

The Kentuckian went down, unconscious, but Eddie didn't know that. He piled on top of the man and tried to kill him. Hildreth was the first one to reach them. He hauled Eddie up and asked without anger, with even a trace of amusement in his tone, "What's the matter here?" And then as he held Eddie, tense and staring down at the prostrate man, Hildreth smelled the whisky. "You trot on back to the house, Eddie. Real quick."

Eddie wrenched away and stalked out of the crowd, going to the barn instead of the house. Jug and Pistol whined at him as he passed, but they were guarding the house and would not leave their posts. By the time Eddie reached the corner of the barn he was sick at his stomach, and even after he emptied it he was still feeling miserable.

He crawled into the meadow hay like a hurt animal. When the dance was over he heard Hildreth coming to him. Hildreth came inside and stood there, his presence heavily felt although unseen; and it was like the night three years before when Eddie would not stay in the house with Captain Walworth.

"You ought to be forgetting some things by now," Hildreth said.

He could not have known the real cause of the outburst tonight; he was guessing on the basis of what he knew of Eddie and he was as close to the truth as Eddie himself could understand it.

"She's a real nice girl, Eddie, but that ain't no way to get along with women, let me tell you."

"I don't want to get along with them."

"A temper is a fine thing," Hildreth said, "but you can't let it run wild, without reason. You know something? We spent an hour bringing that man around, and he's a big, tough fellow. It wasn't funny."

Hildreth went away and presently the dogs came in and bedded down in the hay. To hell with the Kentuckian. And if all Hildreth was going to do from now on was to give advice, Eddie didn't need to stay and hear it.

Soon after daylight the train moved on. Eddie watched them form up and go. Beth came past on the seat of a strong Conestoga, driving while her mother held a crying child. The mother looked down and frowned darkly at Eddie. Beth's expression was serious and disapproving too; but when the wagon had gone past, she turned suddenly and waved at Eddie, a tall, green-eyed girl going westward in the dust.

Something caught in Eddie's throat and he was no longer angry at Beth, or even at the Kentuckian; but when he thought to wave at her, the dust had obscured the wagon. The train crawled out of the valley and out of sight, and out of Eddie Cushman's life forever.

When he turned to go back to work, this place where he had lived three years was bleak and lonely. The old squaws who helped Mrs. Hildreth about the place were going to the creek for water, ugly, unhurried, hopeless like the land.

CHAPTER FOUR

WAR TALK was strong among the people in the last trains that stopped at the trading post in the summer of 1858. Sure as the world, war was going to pop between the North and the South and it would be a hell of a thing too, but the way some of those Southern Congressmen were acting, it looked as if things had gone too far to smooth over.

Eddie took no interest in the talk. He was against slavery because Rumsey Snelling had been for it, but that was as far as he cared to investigate the problem.

Fall closed out emigrant travel on the trail. Jeremy Flint, who freighted goods and supplies to isolated places like the post in Ruby Valley, was due back from California with a drive of mules he intended to sell or trade in the Mormon settlements; but after that there was no certainty that anyone would be along till the middle of spring.

Then Captain Walworth came past with six officers. He and the rest had been ordered to report to Washington, D.C., for new assignments. They were traveling at their own expense and cursing every minute of it.

But Walworth was enthusiastic about the promise of action if war broke out in the States. It turned out that he was an abolitionist. "We'll ride with hell and the sword clean through the South! It's time the slavery question was settled for good!"

"Happens I'm from Missouri," Hildreth said mildly, "and my Pappy never owned no slaves to speak of, but I think I kind of understand the situation. It ain't as bad as some of you fellows make out, and when it comes to riding through the South with hell and the sword, I ain't sure you'll ride too far at one whack."

"We'll see, we'll see," Captain Walworth said. He looked up the valley. "If it does head up like it's threatening to, there won't be many soldiers left out here, Sam. Sko-kup or some other ratty chief just might get it in his head to gobble up places like yours."

Hildreth grinned. "I don't hardly think so, but if it happens, it happens. Me and Eddie ain't fretting none in advance."

The officers left the next day, somewhat unsteady from being up half the night drinking Hildreth's whisky.

"It'll take a war for them to get any promotion," Hildreth said. "Walworth's been a captain for ten years. Let 'em have their war. I was with Doniphan when we stole Texas from the Mexicans, and I had all the marching and fighting I want for the rest of my life." He grinned at the dust of the army men. "Let's go hunting."

High in the Ruby Mountains near a small lake, Eddie sat with Hildreth under a tree and looked on the country below and held in his mind the same perspective of the valley that the view gave: it was a small, unimportant place. The railroad that the old guide had talked about would never come here. Nothing would ever change in this place.

Eddie looked far into the distance, toward Gravelly Crossing, and all the loneliness that he could not shed came over him.

It was time for him to leave. He would go somewhere far away, where it would be possible to forget. For a long time he had been building up to it and now he wanted to tell Hildreth, who sat half drowsing with his rifle across his legs.

Hildreth liked the country. The trading post, although he ran it well, was only his excuse to be here and to stay here. He had found some kind of contentment that could never be for Eddie Cushman in this land.

It was hard to speak of the subject of leaving but Eddie knew that he was going to do so. He rose and stood with his rifle at his side, staring out on the hazy, endless space beyond the small valley.

He said, "Have you ever thought of leaving here, Sam, going on to California, or someplace?"

Hildreth looked up slowly from under his heavy brows. "I thought of it, yes. If Bess and me had kids, maybe we wouldn't have stayed here. But now we've got everything we need, and all the peace you could ask for, so I guess we'll stay."

Until they got old and feeble, or until the Indians went sour and wiped them out. Eddie had learned that death could come quickly. People died and left nothing behind to mark their going.

"Where do you figure to go, Eddie?" Hildreth asked quietly.

Eddie was on the defensive immediately; he was always like that when anyone touched his thoughts before they were spoken. "I didn't say I was going anywhere."

"You've been coming to it for some time. It's natural, I guess." Hildreth ran his hand along the stock of his rifle. "There won't be another train now until—"

"I don't want to go to California or any other place that people kill themselves trying to reach!"

"You're a funny one, Eddie. You're holding too much inside you yet."

Eddie didn't answer. He kept staring at space and the blue skies that ran to the end of the world.

"Jeremy Flint will be back one of these days," Hildreth said. "You could go as far as the Mormon settlements with him this winter."

"That'll be a start." Eddie had wanted to work into his announcement of leaving the fact that he was grateful for all the Hildreths had done for him, but now the thought was driven under a defensive layer because Hildreth had divined his intention of going away before Eddie mentioned it.

Hildreth got up slowly. "Not much use to hunt any more this time, I guess."

It would be the last time for the two of them, Eddie knew. Suddenly he recognized the disparity in their ages. There were touches of gray in Hildreth's beard, and his eyes held a sort of tired and distant expression. Eddie remembered some of the many things the man had done for him, his patience and understanding with the shocked boy of three years ago.

It was time to speak of that, but Eddie didn't know how to go about it.

They gathered up their gear and started back to the valley.

Bess Hildreth heard the news of Eddie's decision to leave when he and Hildreth came in long after dark. "That's the way of boys, I suppose," she said briskly, and turned to the fireplace where she was warming a pot of stew on a swinging hook. She knelt there with her back to Eddie and Hildreth for a long time, dipping into the stew with a long ladle. When she dished up the meat her face was quiet and composed, but Eddie saw Hildreth watching her intently, and saw the faint expression of pain that came to the older man's face as he read his wife's thoughts.

Over a period of several days Hildreth made certain gifts to Eddie. He gave him a tough pony and a saddle the first day.

"I'll send the money back. How much?" Eddie asked.

Hildreth came close to losing his temper. "Don't be a proud fool! Whatever I give you, you've more than earned."

Eddie resolved that he would pay anyway, when he made the money; but he argued no more with Hildreth, who a day or two later gave him a rifle much better than the battered weapon Eddie had carried up the Humboldt. The next day Hildreth gave him a heavy Navy pistol. By degrees Sam Hildreth did his best to equip a young man going out into a wild country.

And then, knowing that material gifts would not solve the larger problem of Eddie Cushman, Hildreth gave advice. "Watch your damned pride and your temper. Remember, in spite of what happened to you a few years ago, there's a lot of love in this world if you're willing to make the exchange." He stared at Eddie moodily and walked away.

The dust of Flint's mule herd was in the valley before Hildreth gave Eddie some news. "When Captain Walworth was here the first time you saw him, I asked him to try to get word to your kin back in Illinois."

"How'd you know where we lived back there?"

"Your folks stopped here three days, Eddie. I talked to your father and mother." Hildreth paused. "It took a year for the message to get back there, but it finally did, and an answer came back. Your grandparents are both dead. They died last summer."

It was old news, of something that had happened long ago. Eddie wondered why it should strike him so hard now, but he covered his feelings and asked, "When did you hear?"

"The first train that came through this summer. I thought the longer I waited the better it would be. Maybe I was wrong. Do you think so?"

"They were awful old when I saw them last." Eddie was choked up. "It's all right." He was not the man he thought he was: he was a little boy again standing in the sun at Gravelly Crossing, with his arm around Kathy, and Mrs. Snelling was looking at them from under the wagon bow. He swallowed and looked at the dust of the mule drive.

Hildreth said nothing as they waited.

At last Eddie thought that his voice would be under control. He said, "Looks like Flint is short of help," and his voice was all right.

"Yeah, it does," Hildreth agreed.

"Let me talk to him, instead of you asking him if I can go with him."

"Sure."

Jeremy Flint was a swarthy, sun-scorched, ragged little man with a round black beard. There was a New England twang in his voice and a trader's shrewdness in his heart. At critical bargaining points of a conversation he had a habit of opening his mouth as if to speak forcefully, then clamping his lips together, and striding away with a shake of his head; but he always returned.

He came into Ruby Valley with seventy head of big California mules, two Mexican riders who were scarcely more than boys, and an old rider named Sonoma. Hildreth asked him how the trip had been.

"Just fine," Jeremy said. "Two lazy riders quit me on the Truckee, the Paiutes stuck arrows into six of my best mules at Big Meadows, Sonoma is talking of quitting, and I probably won't make a cent for all my grief by the time the Saints get through out-trading me. Yes, I'm having a fine trip."

"I feel sorry for you," Hildreth said. "Come and have a drink."

"Free?"

"Anyway, the first one."

"One's all I ever take."

Sonoma was going to quit, all right. Privately, he complained to Eddie about the cold, the distance, the drabness of the country. Sonoma had never been over the Sierras before.

"It's worse east of here," Eddie said.

"It couldn't be," Sonoma said, "but I don't think I'll find out. I should have quit on the Truckee with them others."

Jeremy rested his mules for three days. On the day before he was to leave he came to Eddie and said, "Ever think about having some fun for yourself and making a few dollars?"

"Can't say that I have. What kind of fun?"

"Helping me drive the mules to the Mormon settlements. I really don't need another hand, but I thought it would be an interesting trip for you. Your pa says you can go if you want to."

"How much?" Eddie asked.

"I figured I could give you a mule. You could trade it off and make yourself some real money."

"You said you were going to lose money on the herd," Eddie said.

"And I will, but you can't lose because the mule ain't costing you anything to start with."

"Just a trip across the salt desert. I might consider it for five mules."

Jeremy opened his mouth, closed it and walked away. It appeared that he was going to walk out of the valley but he came back after a time and said, "Two mules then, and that, by God, will ruin me!"

They settled on three mules. Jeremy was woefully short-handed, and knew it. . . .

When Flint saw how quickly Eddie assembled his gear

for the trip, the trader's little eyes sparkled. "I been took. You figured to go with me all the time."

"It's still three mules," Eddie said.

The drive did not start as easily as Eddie had thought it would. The mules gave them the devil's own time about being driven from the valley. It was long after sunup when the herd was at last lined out. Hildreth had helped round up the mules. Now he rode close to Eddie and said, "Good luck, boy." He went back and dismounted where Mrs. Hildreth was standing.

Eddie had told her good-by before he saddled up. It did not seem to be enough now. He waved and Hildreth must have known it was for his wife, not him. Mrs. Hildreth waved back. It was still not enough. Leaving, Eddie knew that he had been too late trying to express his feelings for the Hildreths. There had been too much acceptance on his part and no giving at all. Sure, he had earned his way. He meant to earn his way wherever he went. He had worked hard for Sam Hildreth.

But that much the Hildreths could have bought from someone else. Someone like Sonoma, who was going to stay the winter with them.

Eddie knew that if he had worked ten times as hard as he had, there was still some failure in his relationship with the Hildreths, something he had refused to give them.

Now it was too late.

The mules kicked dust on Eddie. They bit at each other and kicked and grunted. They started with a rush, then settled down to their own pace. Dust devils spun along the lower edges of the hills. Winter was in the air.

The buildings in the valley were flattened and lonely-looking when Eddie turned. The Hildreths had gone inside. Eddie saw the dogs cross the yard and disappear.

Four or five big stripers broke from the herd and started somewhere on a caper of their own. Eddie was slow to move. Flint came pounding through the dust on his wicked little Mexican pony and went after the erring mules.

Dust rolled between Eddie and his last long look at the valley. He was alone with the realization that there is no going back to recapture thoughts unsaid, to do things left undone.

Flint came riding back. "If you're going to earn your keep, stop gawking around and pay attention to things!"

Eddie knew he had left home.

CHAPTER FIVE

Salt-burned and whipped to darkness by the long desert winds, Eddie came into the valley of the Great Salt Lake on a cold, clear day. His willingness to work and his taciturnity had earned him a measure of respect from Jeremy, although the man was careful not to admit it in words. It was enough for Eddie to know that he had done his job well; he expected nothing more than his bargained payment.

No one rushed either to buy the mules or to trade for them. It was winter. Unperturbed, Jeremy camped on the Jordan River and settled down to wait until spring, when the market for his mules would be much better.

After a restless two weeks Eddie said, "I'm going to take my three mules and try some of the settlements south of here."

Jeremy considered the idea for a time. "Might be worth a try. Take three of mine too and see what kind of business you can do." And then he gave Eddie some advice. "You're young. These Mormons are hard traders. Don't let 'em get ahead of you."

Alone, Eddie went south to Spanish Fork. It was a straggling town with a street as wide as any in Salt Lake. He did not get any satisfactory offers for his mules there, so he scouted the country roundabout. It seemed that hay was more in demand than mules, which seemed strange because he saw no lack of hay anywhere.

Bishop Southcott, a bearded, portly man with twinkling eyes, explained the situation. "Along toward spring we run pretty short of hay, son. We've been so busy building canals and ditches that we don't have time to cut and store it, as we will later on."

The bishop himself had a dozen stacks of hay, four of the largest ones grouped close to his house and outbuildings. Along about spring he must make himself some money, Eddie figured. Still, it was darned strange that hay should be short in the fertile bottoms.

Eddie inquired around. Everyone told him that indeed

the bishop spoke the truth: later on the shortage of hay caused no end of trouble. Of course it wouldn't always be that way. Eddie thought it over; he didn't want to appear overanxious to trade off the mules. In time he went to Bishop Southcott, who had shown some interest in the mules, and offered to trade them for six stacks of hay.

The bishop laughed heartily. "You're asking for solid gold in place of those mules, Eddie." He shook his head. "Six stacks of hay! I'll say you're a real trader, son."

Eddie knew he was on the right track, so he tried to act like Jeremy. "I wouldn't have no way to haul it to anyone who wanted to buy it, anyway." He started to walk away.

The bishop had five sons. They all watched their father.

"Now if you were to suggest something reasonable," Bishop Southcott said, "we might get along. Say, about two stacks of hay for—"

"No way for me to haul it." Eddie kept walking.

"You don't have to worry about that," one of the bishop's sons said. "If Pa was foolish enough to trade you hay, there's plenty of folks willing to pay you for it right in the stacks."

"That's a fact," the bishop said. "Come into the house, Eddie, and we'll have some buttermilk and talk about it."

In the end Eddie traded the six mules for four stacks of hay, he himself to pick the four stacks, with the agreement that he could choose only one of the group close to the house. He ate dinner with the Southcotts. They were a fine, religious family and they showed high respect for the father, Eddie thought.

He delivered the mules that afternoon, and then he rode out into the valley to talk to some of the people who had first told him about the shortage of hay. Some of them said that they figured the spring was not going to be as severe as previous ones, that they did not intend to buy hay until they actually needed it.

Others said they had no money, or that they had already made arrangements to buy hay from neighbors.

The demand for hay had vanished suddenly. Eddie went back to his camp on the edge of town.

Billy Bodega was sitting there under a cottonwood, picking his teeth with a splinter. Eddie knew him by sight, a man who had a shack at the lower end of the street, where he gambled with Indians and Gentiles. Bodega was a dark, curly-headed man with a wide grin and sharp brown eyes.

He said, "Find any buyers for the hay?"

Eddie gave him a bitter look. "How'd you know?"

"Everyone does. More Saints than you'd think sneak into my place for a little game now and then."

Eddie sat down on a stump. He needed advice and he needed help, but he wasn't going to ask for either.

"All these places were settled by congregations," Bodega said. "They saw you coming with those mules, particularly after Southcott passed on the word." He watched Eddie steadily. "You've been hoodwinked."

Eddie knew it. He was in a rage against himself for being a fool. Worst of all, he had allowed himself to be cheated out of the three mules Jeremy had entrusted to him for sale or trade. "You wouldn't think a bishop would do that. A bishop of a church!"

"We did worse than that to the Mormons back in Illinois and Missouri, Eddie."

"Not me! I didn't do anything to them!"

"You're still a Gentile out here," Bodega said. "Were all of them your mules?"

"Three of them." Eddie got up and looked at his pistol, checking the loads.

"Don't be a fool. You haven't a chance of getting them back. You'd better go on home and— Where'd you come from, by the way?"

"Clear across the salt desert." Freezing, thirsting, choking on dust. "Is Southcott really a bishop?"

Bodega nodded. He watched Eddie narrowly. "He's the big power around here. Put the pistol away and go home."

"I'll leave when I have the mules."

Bodega made a quick judgment. For a gambler, he appeared startled. "I believe you mean that. How old are you?"

Eddie didn't answer. After a time he put his pistol away and began to cook supper.

Bodega was alone in his shack the next morning. "I'd like an empty whisky bottle, Bodega."

"Sure." Bodega glanced around with a pained expression at the disorder of the room. Behind the curtain of a corner shelf he found a quart bottle with about three drinks in it. He drank the whisky in one long motion, put the cork in the neck, and gave the bottle to Eddie, who started out.

"What are you going to put in it?" Bodega asked.

"Coal oil."

"Don't be fool enough to buy it at the store."

Eddie stopped and turned around.

"I've about run out my usefulness here," Bodega said. "I was about to move on anyway." He grinned, lights sparkling in his brown eyes. "Fill it from the lamp there." He began to throw personal items into saddlebags. "Mind if I watch the performance?"

"It ain't your business."

"If I had stuck to my own business, I'd still be reading law in my father's office in Pennsylvania. Ever been back there, Eddie?"

Eddie corked the bottle and wiped his hands on his pants. "No."

"I found it dull. Just hold up there a minute or two and I'll be with you."

They rode out together to Bishop Southcott's house. Eddie said, "This ain't none of your business, Bodega."

"It sure isn't," Bodega answered cheerfully.

The bishop came from the house with two of his sons. He stroked his beard and his eyes twinkled up at Eddie. "Did you find some hay buyers, son?"

"Decided to keep the hay myself," Eddie said.

The bishop was at once puzzled and wary. The humor left his eyes and he looked at his sons.

Eddie nodded toward the four stacks of hay close to the buildings. "That one on the northeast corner is mine."

The bishop said, "Yes—"

"I've come after it."

Eddie rode over and tossed the bottle of coal oil against the base of the stack. He got down and drew his pistol and with a careful shot smashed the bottle. He pulled a tarred rag from his saddlebags and lit it.

The bishop and his sons came on the run. "Have you gone crazy?" Southcott shouted.

"My stack of hay."

"You can't burn it! Good Lord, boy, this close to my house and all—"

"You traded me the stack of hay. You said it was mine."

One of the bishop's sons started back toward the house.

Eddie fired into the ground ahead of him. "Come back here." The youth obeyed.

The tarred rag was catching fully now. Eddie dropped it and picked it up with a stick.

"You're nothing but a Gentile thug!" the bishop raged.

"You're a bishop," Eddie said. "You ought to know better than to cheat. Put the mules out in the lane before this rag burns away."

"I will not!"

Eddie walked closer to the stack of hay.

"You'd better do it, Southcott," Bodega said. "He's not bluffing."

The bishop gave Bodega the edge of his anger. "You gambling son of satan, I'll remember you for this!"

"Yes, sir," Bodega answered, "but you'd better get the mules out of the barn first."

The bishop watched Eddie's bitter, steady expression. "You young criminal!"

Part of the burning rag dropped to the ground. Eddie walked closer to the stack and Southcott watched the wind laying the black smoke directly toward his buildings. He began to shout at his sons to drive the mules out of the barn.

He was standing in the yard with his fist raised and his beard jerking to his wrathful curses as Eddie and Bodega drove the six mules away.

Bodega was laughing, but after a time he stopped and looked at Eddie strangely. They went at a fast clip back toward the road to Salt Lake. Bodega asked, "What's the matter, didn't you get any fun out of it?"

"I didn't go there for fun. I went there to get the mules."

"You're a strange kid, Eddie." Bodega shook his head. "No, you're not a kid."

They rode with little rest until they reached Jeremy's camp on the Jordan. The trader said, "No good down that way, huh?"

"No good," Eddie answered.

Two weeks later he traded his three mules for gold and a stout gray horse to a man in a wagon train that had stopped to winter in the valley. With Bodega and Pete Cleveland, a former soldier of the Mormon battalion who had not found life in Deseret to his liking, Eddie set out to go to New Mexico Territory.

Jeremy Flint was sorry to see Eddie leave, although he did not say so. He asked, "What'll I tell the Hildreths?"

"Nothing. I'll write 'em." Eddie intended to, but he never did; the years separated the layers of his intentions. He rode away with Bodega and Cleveland and before he had gone a hundred yards he knew how much he liked Jeremy Flint.

Eddie looked back. Flint was standing beside a mule, watching the three riders. Eddie raised his hand. Jeremy gave him a small wave in return and then stooped to raise the foreleg of the mule.

Pete Cleveland was as reckless and full of laughter as Bodega. They made a long holiday of a trip that was a grim trail to most men. Eddie liked to hear their laughter but he never knew how to join them in it, and he fretted silently because they were never in a hurry. He himself was in a great hurry to get to New Mexico, because he hoped to find something there, although he did not know what it was.

Whatever it was, he did not find it. Once more, when he parted with Bodega and Cleveland a week after reaching Santa Fe, he knew he had liked them, too.

CHAPTER SIX

In 1870 there was little outward resemblance in Ed Cushman to the boy who had ridden away from Ruby Valley. He had wandered far. He had been touched briefly by the Civil War. He had rubbed shoulders with all kinds of men and learned the general patterns of their natures, and he had been suspicious of them all the time.

He was riding now on the highlands of the Arkansas Valley with a pack horse and six steers that he had wintered in the warm Greenhorn country. The snow was melting where he rode but the mountains on his left were still deep in winter.

Some thirty miles ahead was the camp of Victory. Before the war the gulch had been barely touched but since last summer it had been renamed and was going strong, according to Cushman's information. He had heard that a hard core of about twenty-five miners had stayed in the camp all winter, fighting snow and cold and pneumonia and frozen ground. By now they should be hungry enough to pay well for fresh beef.

There were ranches in the valley, set on the lee side of hills where great grass bottoms flowed down from the mountains. The cattle on them seemed to have wintered well enough, but unless things had changed since the war, Cushman knew the ranchers were not particularly interested in driving through the snow to isolated mining camps.

He stopped at none of the ranches, but grazed his steers in late afternoon close to the river, where the sun had uncovered rich pockets of last year's grass. He was in no great hurry, confident that he was the first man up the river with beef.

At twenty-eight Ed Cushman was a rangy, big-boned man whose gray eyes looked coldly on the world. In moments of relaxation, which came only when there was no other human being near, his expression sometimes took on a puzzled, brooding look, as if he didn't know what it was he sought. It wasn't wealth, he knew, because twice he had been quite close to riches before they faded away like wind on the desert; but there had been no real satisfaction even when the prospects seemed assured.

He had no desire for power, for that meant close and continual residence with other men. Once he had been a deputy sheriff in a New Mexico cattle town, and although he had performed as he was supposed to do, risking his life when called upon to do so, taking a wound that had left one lower arm slightly crooked, and killing two men in the name of the law, he had been thoroughly disgusted with the office and had quit it after three months.

He didn't know what he wanted from life, except that there was some drive in him that told him if he kept going long enough and far enough, he might some day find an answer to the loneliness that had grown in him.

He made his camp beside the cold Arkansas, putting himself between his animals and the easy passage up a gulch to the high west bank of the river. The bent brown grasses of last fall were thick enough for the horses and steers to forage all night if they cared to.

For a while after dark he sat beside his small fire, listening to the endless movement of the water on worn rocks.

He thought of the Hildreths; their faces were hazy in his memory, but he could recall clearly the kind of people they had been and how, too late, he had understood their qualities. Even in the matter of going-away gifts, Hildreth had been wise and kind.

If he had made the gifts all at one stroke, Cushman would have been forced to expressions of gratitude that would have embarrassed him; but Hildreth had spread out his kindness day by day, so that each part was accepted easily, and that was the way he had treated Cushman in all things. Looking back, one could understand the whole. Sam Hildreth had been a rare man in that he did not want appreciation. Cushman had never met another like him.

Long ago, Cushman thought . . . damnation to long ago; there must be something waiting on ahead. He rose and put out the fire and stood looking into the darkness across the river, knowing that the next day would be another lonely searching for something unknown, on top of thousands of other days just like it.

He heard the man coming in the bitter reaches of the cold night, a clumsy man who left his horse on the high bank and came thumping down toward the camp. Bright moonlight was striking a cold sheen on the river and making queer shadows on the cliffs across the water.

Cushman got out of his blankets and stood in the shadows with his rifle.

The man, squat and bearded, stumbled into the camp before he knew he was upon it. He stood there in a stupid pose, peering around uncertainly. "Hey! Anyone here?"

Cushman kept listening for noises up on the bank. He heard none. "What do you want?" he asked from the darkness. The man swung around with a gasp.

The fellow peered toward Cushman. "Where are you?"

"What do you want?"

"I'm Joe Kenton. I'm looking for help. We got a wagon stuck upstream in the river."

"When did you get stuck?"

"Just about sundown, up at the crossing below Trout Creek. She's afraid the water will come up and—"

"The water ain't coming up for a while," Cushman said. "How'd you find me?"

"I was riding for help at some ranch. I seen the tracks

of your horses and thought there must be a house down here."

"You're alone?"

"Why, sure." Kenton shifted around uneasily, trying to see from the moonlight into the dark by the rock where Cushman was.

Cushman said, "I'll be coming up the river tomorrow," neither giving nor withholding a promise of help.

"She wanted to get out of there tonight."

Some outfit with ten kids, Cushman thought; and it was a full two months early for a wagon to be in this part of the mountains. He thought of the Snellings, letting everyone else pick up their mistakes for them. "I'll be up that way tomorrow sometime," he said.

"We can pay you for your trouble. It ain't so awful far, and the moonlight makes it easy riding. If—"

"I'm going nowhere tonight," Cushman said. "Now get out of my camp and let me sleep."

Kenton stood where he was. He said stubbornly, "If the river comes up in the meantime—"

"It won't raise an inch. Now get out."

Kenton let his breath out with a heavy grunting sound. "How far is it to a ranch?"

"Four, five miles." Cushman was tired of the man. First, he stuck a wagon at an easy crossing, and then he let a woman drive him out in the freezing night to put upon other people for help. Let him go on to a ranch, if he thought anyone was idiot enough to get out of bed in the middle of the night to help him.

Kenton turned away and started back up the gulch, walking with a heavy, pigeon-toed movement. His frozen pants legs rasped together as he went.

"In spite of the moonlight, you're going to have a hard time finding a ranch house," Cushman said. "They're all tucked in pretty snug in the cottonwoods under the hills."

Kenton didn't answer. Cushman heard him go on up the bank and mount. The man didn't ride away immediately. His horse stamped restlessly and Kenton stayed on the bank, apparently trying to make up his mind.

After a few minutes he rode away.

Cushman walked up the gulch to make sure. Kenton was going up-river. It was bitterly cold. Cushman went back to his camp. He knew the crossing; it was easy. Some of these hopeless people should have seen the Missouri in full flood. He stood by the dead fire and old memories came out of the night.

They pursued him after he got back into his blankets. He remembered the crashing instant when he had last seen Billy Bodega. He had gone across the Rio Grande with Captain Dodd's company to support the Union guns at Val Verde. Out of the dust and the quivering shouts there came the thunder of the first charge of Texan lancers.

Dodd's company beat them back. Dodd's company almost destroyed the lancers, but they kept coming. There was one stark moment when Cushman saw Bodega, leaning forward on his horse, his mouth wide open with shouting, bearing straight toward Cushman with his pistol raised.

In that tick of time they recognized each other. Bodega swerved off to the left. Cushman fired his rifle into the dust behind Bodega. It was one clear instant, and after that there was only confusion and shouting and dust around the guns. Captain McRae lost his battery and the Union men fell back across the river and Cushman never knew whether or not Bodega had come out of the charge alive.

When he least expected it, Cushman's mind was suddenly taken with these flashing, disturbing memories of the past. There was no reason that he could understand why Kenton's coming to the camp should have started the somber train of remembrance again, but it was so.

Before sunup Cushman was on the move. The hoofs of the steers clacked on the frozen ground as the animals went reluctantly into the icy edge of the northern wind. After an hour the wind died and the sun grew warm and there was a rising brownness all over the floor of the valley between the patches of coarse snow, but the sheer mountains ahead and on the left still held their eye-shattering whiteness.

By late afternoon the river might rise a little. If the wagon up ahead was not out by the time Cushman got to it, he supposed he would have to give the blundering fools a hand.

He turned with the river and saw the gentle run of hills where Trout Creek Pass came down. After a time he turned north once more, fording the river where it was wide and shallow. Two miles beyond, on the mesa, he came to the track of a wagon that had come off the pass

the day before. It had gone angling toward the bloom
of cottonwoods along the Arkansas. He stared down at the
divided marks of oxen shoes. For a long time he had hated
oxen.

Reluctantly he followed the wagon trail to the river.
It had gone down an easy slope to the water, and on the
other side there was a simple way up; but the driver
had disregarded, or overlooked, tiny swirls that meant a
bottom of jagged rocks. Although it was not even hub-
deep in the stream, the wagon was badly hung up.

On the far bank Cushman saw smoke. He looked downstream for an easy crossing for the steers. It was there, a
shallow riffle breaking over solid gravel, not a hundred
yards from where the wagon was jammed. He eyed the
conveyance sourly. It was bigger than it should have been,
higher too, a top-heavy affair with a stovepipe sticking
through a metal square in the canvas.

Some idiot was trying to travel in the mountains with all
the comforts of home.

Cushman went down and crossed the steers below the
grove of cottonwoods. He unsaddled the pack horse and
took all the rope he had and went on into the grove.

Kenton and a woman were standing near a fire, soaked
to the waists. Stacked around the grove were cases and
boxes and gear they had carried from the wagon. Cushman
knew that he had estimated Kenton accurately. The man
was squat and powerfully built. He was also slow and not
very smart; the wagon itself was evidence of that.

The woman puzzled Cushman. She didn't belong with
Kenton. She was no girl by any means; Cushman estimated
that she was in her mid-twenties, tall and strongly formed,
with a set to her neck and back that spoke of pride and
determination. Her hair was a rich brown color, tied at
the back with a black grosgrain ribbon. It appeared that
she had combed it back straight and hard this morning,
with no regard for appearance, but now it had strayed
back in a natural heavy waviness and some of it was straggling down one cheek. Her mouth was full and wide.

She looked steadily at Cushman and he received the
impression of sharply upslanted eyebrows, but as he stared
at her, he decided that it was the set of her eyes, rather
than the brows, that gave the impression. In the conventional sense she could not be called beautiful, Cushman
thought; there was too much of an air of strength and

will about her for that. But she didn't belong out here beside a wagon stuck in a river.

"Is this the man you talked to last night?" she asked Kenton.

Her voice was smoothly controlled. Cushman would have described it as carrying a tone of culture and breeding, of coming from a background of life strange to him. In a way it reminded him of Billy Bodega's voice. Bodega the gambler, the son of an Eastern judge. Billy Bodega was not his name; he had picked it up because the sound pleased him. He had poked fun at his own background, but his voice had always been softly toned, superior, as if he were poking fun, too, at everyone else's background.

This woman, standing beside a fire with her dress soaked and draped to the shape of her body, asked stupid-looking Joe Kenton a question that seemed designed to put Cushman in his place before he had a chance to speak.

"Yeah, that's him," Kenton said.

"I didn't send my driver down the river for help from you or anyone else," the woman said. "I mentioned that the river might rise, although I have no fear that it will before we're out of it. Mr. Kenton became worried and rode away without my bidding."

"All right." Cushman didn't like the imperiousness or the air of self-sufficiency about the woman. She acted as if she was in her own mansion back wherever she came from, explaining something to servants. He looked at the wagon. By taking off one rear wheel and lashing a heavy skid in its place, they probably could drag the heavy vehicle over the main rock that had it fouled, and after that it ought to come clear with the oxen and his two horses hauling away.

He rode to the edge of the river for a look. If they swung hard downstream right after clearing that one bad rock, it wouldn't be bad. The thing of it was, you had to stagger around on slippery rocks, belly-deep in icy water, to remove one rear wheel and get a skid in place, all because this grand dame didn't have brains enough to hire a driver with common sense.

Cushman watched the river breaking through the wheel spokes and rippling over the big rock. You wouldn't have to lash the skid to the axle, as he'd first planned. You could use a small tree as a skid on which to drag the wagon up on the rock, then put the wheel back on. Hell, it wouldn't be too bad, after all, except the cold soaking in the river.

He felt better, at least about the work involved. "What kind of a rig is that, anyway?" he asked.

"It's a restaurant," Kenton said proudly. "You haul it to one camp, stove and everything, and then if business ain't—"

"Never mind, Mr. Kenton," the woman said. "I'm sure the gentleman is more interested in going on about his business than hearing of ours."

"I am, for a fact," Cushman said, "but I'll help you get the wagon out." He looked hard at the woman. She wasn't going to get on very well in this country with an attitude like hers.

"That won't be necessary."

Her coolness irritated Cushman more than he would have admitted. "I was camped last night when your man showed up. There was no sense in getting out because there was nothing we could have done in the dark. That's what's sticking in your craw, isn't it?"

"Not at all," the woman said. She looked at Cushman as if he were a child. "I quite agree that nothing could have been done last night, and I've already told you that I didn't send Mr. Kenton for help." She came to the edge of the river and looked at the wagon without alarm.

Her skin was smooth and faintly dusky from the sun. Her eyes were green and calm. For all her high airs, Cushman had to admire her composure. So she was going to run a restaurant in the wagon, moving from one camp to another if business didn't suit her in any one location. She had an idea, at that, and looked as if she had the courage to carry it out.

"How many oxen have you got?" Cushman asked.

"Six. And a good horse." The woman inclined her head toward the cottonwoods. It was the first unladylike gesture Cushman had seen her make.

"That's enough to get the wagon," he said. "Where's your ax? Let's get started."

"How much will you charge?"

"Look," Cushman said "you're stuck in the river. I'll help you get clear. That's all there is to it."

"How much will you charge?"

"Nothing! Let's get the job done and let me get on my way to Victory."

"I'll pay you ten dollars."

Cushman had offered his help, grudgingly, to be sure. If there had been two men here, they could have gone to hell for all the help he would have given. Now, by insisting on paying him, the woman was making him feel his own attitude keenly. He didn't like it.

"Do you want me to help you get the wagon out—for nothing?" he asked.

"No," the woman said quietly, "I don't. How much more do you want?"

Cushman walked to his horse and mounted. He expected the woman to say, "Wait a minute." She didn't even look at him.

Kenton, who had been standing with his head moving from side to side as he followed the conversation, was the one who protested. "Hold on, Miss Drago! I don't think I can—"

"You got it in there. I think you can get it out," the woman said. "If not, you can go to a ranch down the valley and hire help."

Cushman hesitated a moment longer. Kenton stared at him helplessly, and then the man's expression changed to solid anger. "You dirty, selfish, backbiting—" For all his clumsiness, Kenton was swift as he leaped toward a rifle leaning against a stack of cases.

"No, Mr. Kenton," the woman said unhurriedly. "Let the gentleman go without further argument."

Cushman rode away. He kept one eye on Kenton, but there was no need. Kenton's motion, when his hand was almost on the rifle, was stopped as if by a wall. He turned slowly and put a murderous look on Cushman. Miss Drago glanced at neither man. She said, "Now, Mr. Kenton, let's figure some way to get the wagon out before this warm day brings the water up."

A few minutes before, Cushman would have interpreted her mention of rising water as an indirect appeal for help, and even now it could have been taken as a slap at his stubbornness; but he knew it was neither. Miss Drago simply had forgotten him and was stating a fact.

Cushman put the saddle and gear back on the pack horse. He rounded up his steers and drove them around the grove and on up to the next gravel bench. He held close to the high bank of the river where the swatches of snow were melting fast under the warm spring sun. From a quarter of a mile away he looked back and saw the wagon.

Kenton was leading a span of oxen out to it. The sun struck on the white water breaking around their legs. The animals were bellowing at the cold. Sheer force used to try to drag the wagon free would result in a broken wheel, tip that fancy stove over, and pry up hell in general.

Cushman stopped his horse, frowning as he looked back on the scene. Miss Drago came to the edge of the river, a small figure struggling with a cottonwood log dragged by one end.

Maybe she had the right idea about getting the wagon out. It would have to be her idea; Kenton didn't have sense enough to pour sand from a boot with the directions on the heel. Cushman watched the woman wade out into the river, floating the log below her. She floundered about and almost fell. She pointed for Kenton to go back to the bank, and after a time he got the idea and took the span of oxen to the shore.

Cushman watched the two of them trying to block up the wagon so they could pull a wheel. He knew how numbing the flow of the Arkansas was against their bodies.

The steers drifted on ahead. They were three hundred yards away before Cushman noticed. He rode after them. Damn it, that was the way she wanted it. She was a proud, sure woman, taking nothing from her inferiors. She would have made a hired hand of him, Ed Cushman, who had learned independence the bitter way.

Once more he stopped. If they skidded the wagon too far and let the wheel-less axle drop over the rock, they were in for real trouble. Cushman couldn't see the river now, but he kept looking back toward the bend of the mesa. Kenton might wreck the wagon, get the woman hurt. Cushman cursed the man. He sat for a time longer looking back at the muddy tracks of his passage, and then he turned his horse sharply and rode on to take care of his own affairs.

He knew men who would have laughed at her insistence on paying for help, men who would have extricated the wagon and then said, "Aw, hell, forget it." There would have been no offense, no sensitiveness about being demeaned because the woman had offered to pay.

Cushman went on up the narrowing valley, plopping through the mud, driving his steers slowly. The great snow peaks threw dazzling white against him. He squinted hard as he rode. Muddy rivulets from the melting snow were running toward the river. By late afternoon or evening, if they didn't have the wagon free, the Arkansas could very well take it on down the river.

Only a few times since leaving Ruby Valley had Cushman gone out of his way to volunteer help to someone in a fix. He took care of himself and expected others to do the same. His rebuff at the wagon sat strangely troublesome in his mind.

By late afternoon he was as far north as the camp of Victory, off in the mountains to his left. The short way was a straight line, but he looked at the timbered ridges that lay between him and his destination and knew that the snow would be deep under the trees. There was no great hurry; the miners at Victory would be all the hungrier for beef two or three days from now. He went on up the river, so that he could swing around and come into the wide gulch that led to the camp on the western side of three great ridges interposed between the valley and the steep rise of the mountains proper. In the gulch the sun would have had a chance to do its work and he would not have to fight deep snow under the pines.

Cushman drove his steers along. Several times he was close enough to the river to look down into it. The clear water of this morning was growing roily from the runoff of the snow.

He wondered if the woman and Kenton had got the wagon out all right.

CHAPTER SEVEN

He camped that night near a crude cabin on the Arkansas, where a lonely prospector welcomed him vociferously. The man was young, bearded to the chest. His clothes were patched with buckskin. Out in the river was a gravel bar where he had been sluicing all winter. Cushman asked him how he had done.

"No good at all."

"Then why did you stay?"

The prospector cocked an eye at the river. "Spring floods will bring down the heavy gold. All I got so far is flour stuff, but I'll be here when the heavy water washes the nuggets down. Couldn't take a chance on having someone jump the claim."

Spring floods would bring mud down, Cushman thought. He took care of his horses and set up a camp in a grove of cottonwoods.

The prospector wanted Cushman to share his cabin for the night, a miserable hovel without windows, and with a ridgepole so low that the owner, not a tall man, could not stand erect inside. The fireplace was crudely joined against the logs and smoke blew into the room with every shift of the wind.

Cushman declined to stay there on the pretext that he had to stay outside to watch his steers. The prospector invited him to have supper inside and Cushman countered by asking the man to eat outside with him. He knew by the way the prospector ate that he had been on short rations. The man jammed bacon into his mouth with his fingers and kept watching the steers.

After a time he said, "I'll trade you a tenth interest in my claim for one of them steers, butchered tonight."

"I'm not interested."

"You won't do any better in Victory. When the spring floods come down—"

"I'm not interested in mining at all."

"A quarter share in the claim?"

Cushman shook his head.

"I'll say one half, and after that you can go to hell!" The prospector swabbed grease from the fry pan with a biscuit and kept looking at the steers.

"How many miners stayed in Victory through the winter?" Cushman asked.

"Some, I guess." The prospector kept swabbing at the pan. When the last biscuit was gone he ran his finger through the hardening grease and licked it, and after that he reached out with his tongue, licking at his beard. "I ain't plumb out of grub. I got beans and flour and some other fixin's left, but by God, I'm starved for meat."

"I saw deer along the river all the way up."

"When I was a kid we lived on game too much for me to like it again. It ain't like fresh beef, mister."

"That's right," Cushman said. He watched the hungry

glitter in the prospector's eyes. The man had eaten a fair-sized meal, but he had his mind so set on fresh meat that he didn't realize his belly was full.

"I've got a mighty fine rifle I'll trade you straight across for any steer in that bunch."

"I don't need another rifle."

"Yeah," the prospector said sullenly. "Thanks for the meal." The prospector went back to his cabin.

Cushman moved his bed into the trees. He was in for an uneasy night. There was a faint chance that the prospector might be stunned into solid sleep by the first good meal he'd had in a long time; but Cushman thought otherwise. Experience had taught him that a hungry stomach is likely to be more enraged after a meal. A mind that had lived a long time with even the thought of hunger could not read correctly the signals from the belly.

Cushman did not expect the man so soon. In the first strong grip of early sleep he did not hear the prospector come from his cabin. The horse heard, and grew restless, and that wakened Cushman. Stalking through the moonlight with an ax aslant past his matted beard and hair, the prospector was a wild-looking figure. He was in his bare feet. Great bulges at the knees of his long underwear made his legs appear deformed.

By the time Cushman rolled out and grabbed his rifle, the man had gone into the shadows where the steers were bedded down. Cushman heard one of the animals getting up noisily. If he fired, the whole six of them would go rocketing away and some of them might break their legs on the boulders along the river.

"Drop that ax! I'm centered on you."

Dead silence lay in the shadows where Cushman could not see. He heard another steer rising after a moment.

"Back out of there!"

"Just one," the prospector pleaded from the darkness. "My gut's in a twist for meat."

"Drop the ax and back out of there!"

Cushman heard the ax thump the frozen ground. "I wanted only one!" The prospector ran from the trees and went back to his cabin.

Cushman went out and retrieved the ax. He put his back to a cottonwood and draped his blankets around him. He spent the rest of the night taking short dozes. At times he heard the prospector banging around in his cabin, and once the man came to the door and yelled, "I ought to kill you, you tight son of a bitch! I wanted only one!"

In the morning the prospector came out and went to the river for a bucket of water. For a while he stood looking up to where Cushman was cooking his breakfast. "I hope they all die in the snow before you ever get to Victory."

"I'll take the chance."

The prospector went back to his cabin and closed the door. He had said he still had food, so Cushman let him go. It was not his fault that the man had chosen to stay here and wolf out the winter beside a worthless claim. If he had such a hunger for meat, let him hunt deer in the piñon country across the river.

From the gravel mesa above, while he was driving his steers away, Cushman looked down on the smoke of the cabin. He could not say that the prospector was crazy, for he himself could remember one night on the Humboldt River when the memory of cool, firm apples in his grandfather's orchard had so obsessed him that he had begun to stuff dry grass into his mouth—and the first few frantic bites had actually tasted like apples.

With no quickening of interest because he was getting closer to his immediate destination, Cushman found the wide gulch that led up to Victory. The steers would bring him money, which he would spend drifting on somewhere else until he neded money again. He had no roots anywhere.

Yes, he thought, that unshaved, smelly man in the cabin by the worthless claim was better off than Ed Cushman.

Before long he was into drifts of snow where the wind had coursed across the gulch from the timbered ridges. Over in the trees the snow was three feet deep, but there was good passage in the gulch; Cushman guessed men had gone back and forth, visiting other camps, moving about restlessly even during the strong mountain winter. Between the long curving terraces of the drifts there was often solid ground.

Not hurrying, Cushman made good progress.

There was no forage here, and there would be none at Victory, but that was a worry he could forget now. He would reach the camp some time this afternoon and the steers would be sold and butchered soon afterward. After that he would go somewhere else, probably back down the river to wait for summer. It didn't matter.

He considered reserving one haunch of beef to take back to the prospector; but it was only an idle thought. The man would not understand that it was really not for him, but an effort to pay back a little girl who had given Cushman two biscuits long ago.

The sun was still bright on the high, cold reaches of the mountains when Cushman reached the camp. Victory was in a tree-ringed basin where three small streams came together to form Campanero Creek. Great drifts of snow lay at the upper end of the basin, and in the surrounding timber the snow was deep and soft. Cushman knew it was well that he had not tried to take the short way.

A steady, bitter wind was coming off the mountains. Cushman buttoned his mackinaw. The steers plodded on, following the lead of a big brindle brute who sensed that there should be hay ahead because there were human habitations in sight. For a while the absence of men in view did not strike Cushman. He observed that miners had stirred around mightily during the winter, shoveling snow back from the creek in places, building long, narrow timber shelters over their sluices. Fires were still smoldering where men had been thawing the frozen earth.

Cabins and huts and tents that were stained with age were scattered along the creek and in the edge of the timber, where hard-packed trails led through snow trenches to half-buried habitations. At the upper end of the camp stood the biggest building in the gulch, a long log structure that faced the south. The sun had melted the snow away from that side of it to show the heavy dirt banking around the lower logs. Smoke from a fireplace chimney was drifting along the ridge. Empty whisky kegs, just emerging from a snowdrift at one end of the building, proclaimed the nature of the structure.

Every man in camp must be in the saloon, Cushman thought. He drove his steers a little closer, and then he heard shouts and talking off to the left where one of the branch creeks came in from the south. It sounded like a celebration going on.

He made the turn around a jut of timber and there in a small gulch he saw what was going on. The whole population of Victory was butchering cattle. The snow was red

where they were working. Piles of steaming entrails were
giving vapor into the cold air and men with bloody knives
were chattering like jubilant Indians.

Cushman stopped and stared at the scene. Some rancher
from the valley had beaten him here, coming in by a route
he did not know. There had been no tracks of cattle in the
gulch. So intent were the miners on their work that they
did not see Cushman for a few moments, and then a
bearded giant in a ragged coat and Scotch cap pointed
with a long knife.

"We're being overrun, boys! There's another herd!"

"Hell, we got meat now. What we need is more drinking
whisky."

No rancher had brought the cattle here ahead of Cushman. He knew the truth when he saw squat Joe Kenton
using a horse to help hoist a carcass on a skinning bar
laid between two trees. The slaughtered cattle were the
oxen from the wagon stuck in the Arkansas. Kenton must
have fought like a fiend through the deep snow in the
timber to get them here.

A grinning miner came up to Cushman. "The market
for what you got just busted, brother, but I still might
make you a deal."

"A tenth interest in your claim?"

The miner's eyes widened. "You must have been in a
mining camp before." He scratched his beard. His bright
eyes and shrewd good nature reminded Cushman of
Jeremy Flint, the mule trader. "No, I'll do a little better
than that. For them six beeves I'll trade you a claim at
the upper end of the main gulch. It's under four feet of
snow and ice right now and it may not be worth a damn."

"You trying to back into a deal?" Cushman asked.

"Just telling the truth. There's gold here. There might
be gold on that claim. Again, there might not be."

"What would you do with the steers?"

"Oh, I could find some use for them, I guess."

"I imagine," Cushman said dryly. He estimated the number of men in sight and set the figure at twenty. "In
about two weeks from now when everyone is out of meat,
I guess you could find a use for beef."

"It might be less time than that. Big John over there
swears he can eat a half a steer tonight, but however long
it takes for the first six to disappear, you've still got to
drive your cattle out of here to feed 'em, and then bring

'em back. In the meantime, who knows but what a rancher will show up with a bunch?"

Cushman watched the butchering. The miner was right, and Cushman knew it. Moreover, he'd had enough of nursing steers. There were ways by which he could still come out with a good profit but he didn't care to extend his operation longer. The mining claim might be a good gamble.

Cushman swung down from the horse and stretched his legs. The steers were bawling, nosing the trampled snow for forage. Cushman thought of the ride back to the valley.

"My name's Jake Dunbar," the miner said, "from Illinois four years ago. I'm damned nigh an old-timer out here now."

Cushman introduced himself and they shook hands. He nodded toward the butchering scene. "Did Kenton bring those cattle in here alone?"

"No. That was the biggest surprise of all. We—" Dunbar grabbed at his hat and grinned. "Howdy, Miss Drago, we was about to talk about you."

Cushman swung around and saw the woman. Her heavy woolen skirts were brushing the snow. She wore a woolly white jacket that heightened the clear brown color of her complexion. She gave Dunbar a courteous smile as she came forward. Cushman might not have been there at all. She walked past the two men and stood a short distance ahead, watching the butchering. Joe Kenton, helping now with the skinning of the ox he had hoisted, saw her instantly and paused in his work, looking from her to Cushman.

"No, Kenton didn't come alone," Dunbar said unnecessarily. "She was riding ahead, breaking trail." He watched Miss Drago for a while as she stood tall and straight against the snow. "Now there's real class, Cushman," he murmured.

"This claim you mentioned, Dunbar—I'll give you five steers for it."

Dunbar started to say something. He took a long look at Cushman's face. "You're not one to haggle, are you?"

"That's it. I can butcher those steers and keep the meat in the snow as well as you. That's what you're figuring to do. Sold by the piece, they'll bring more dust than on the hoof."

"Yep!" Dunbar said. "You've just become a claim owner.

I'll throw in a cabin on the deal, or you can stay with me."

"I'll take the cabin."

"Then it's settled. I'll give you a quitclaim deed in the saloon as soon as you want it." Dunbar walked over to the woman. "You'd best get in the clear, miss. We're going to shoot the steers."

The woman walked back toward the camp and stopped. Dunbar drew a pistol. "Give me a hand, Cushman?"

Together they killed four steers with four shots. One of the others whirled and charged toward Miss Drago. She stood her ground calmly and the steer swerved past her, bucketing toward the saloon. The sixth one went down the branch gulch toward the miners. "Go it, you son of a gun!" Dunbar yelled, and fired into the air.

Tail high, bawling, the steer went rampaging toward the twenty miners. They scattered, running toward the trees. One man slipped in his rush to leap into a snowbank. He got up to try again. The steer brushed him with its shoulder and knocked him skidding into a pile of entrails. It charged at three men who were helping each other scramble through the snow. They all went down, yelling and cursing, and the animal swerved away from them.

Kenton leaped toward his sidling horse. He snatched his rifle from the boot. With one shot he piled the steer up dead in the heavy snow at the turn of the gulch.

The miners were bellowing with laughter at the plight of their unfortunate companions. One man had tried to climb a tree. A low limb had broken and plumped him backward into the snow, where he was threshing around in an effort to gain his feet. The one who had been knocked down by the steer was brushing off his clothes with handfuls of snow. He slipped and sat down suddenly on the paunch of one of the oxen.

Jake Dunbar, still holding his pistol, laughed until tears stood on his cold-bright cheeks. When he got himself under control he shoved the pistol under his waistband and yelled down the gulch, "Somebody stick that steer before it freezes!"

A miner yelled back, "I'd rather cut your throat!"

Dunbar began to laugh again. "That's the funniest thing that's happened all winter!"

"You'd better get the other one before it wanders toward

the valley," Cushman said. "I'll stick these four here."

Dunbar studied Cushman's unsmiling expression as if puzzled. He walked away. Before he passed the woman he was laughing again.

Miss Drago came over to Cushman, watching coolly as he bled the steers. For a woman of her breeding, she took it calmly, Cushman thought. She was a cool one all around, grabbing opportunity and making that ride through the snow to beat him here. She knew how to get along in a new country.

"How's the wagon?" he asked.

"It's out, thank you."

Cushman went on with his work. She had stolen a march on him. If he hadn't made that slip about going to Victory there at the river, she might have thought he was going to some more easily reached camp.

The more a man talked . . . Cushman wiped his knife in the snow and stood up, studying her. Well, that was all right. Everyone was in competition with everyone else, in one way or another. Cushman's belief in the competitive principle was so strongly rooted that he felt no resentment about being beaten; but this was the first time a woman had ever outsmarted him.

"Where you from, Miss Drago?"

"From Denver—this trip," she said carefully. Her words, the tone, and the look she gave Cushman closed the door on further questions about her personal life.

A shot sounded over near the saloon as Dunbar killed the last steer.

Dark-faced from the cold, Kenton came up the gulch with his rifle. He gave Cushman a hard look of dislike. "Are you all right, Miss Drago?"

"Of course."

Kenton stared at Cushman. "He should have warned you about getting back when—"

"He did, Mr. Kenton. You can go on back now. Be sure that you get the best possible half of one of the cattle for my share."

"I already done that," Kenton said. The muzzle of his rifle swung across Cushman as he turned to go back to the butchering.

"Where are you from, Mr. Cushman?"

The question surprised Cushman. He answered as the woman had answered. "From the Greenhorns—last trip."

The woman smiled faintly. *"Touché."*

Except for what he had learned from Billy Bodega, Cushman never would have known what she meant. He felt the wide disparity of their backgrounds. He wondered what lay behind this handsome, cool woman that had brought her here. Bodega had been a black sheep and he didn't give a damn; but he was a man and a man can be fondly regarded because of being a black sheep. A woman either conformed or was considered no good.

Ed Cushman studied Miss Drago and did not know what she was.

She asked, "Are you staying here?"

"I might."

"The reason I asked, Mr. Cushman, is that I might be interested in buying your horses. I intend to bring my wagon on up here as soon as possible."

"They're not draught horses, and I'm not interested in selling them."

"Very well." Miss Drago dismissed the subject with a lift of her brows.

Damn her proprietary air. She seemed to think that anything could be bought.

Kenton came by on the horse, dragging a half of beef in the soft snow near the timber. "You want I should hang it up in a tree behind your cabin, Miss Drago?"

"That will do for the time being."

So she had a cabin, Cushman thought. She was going to settle right down.

Miners began to stream past, carrying various pieces of beef chopped from the oxen carcasses with axes. They were mostly bearded men, their cheeks and foreheads burned from the strike of sun on snow. They were tough, healthy men. And they were all young, or they wouldn't have been here.

Some of them took time to touch their hats and greet the woman. Others merely looked and went on by, and afterward raucous laughter broke out among small groups of them.

They had been here all winter with snow and wind and drudgery. Other appetites beside craving for fresh meat had been sharpened by their exile. One lone woman in camp . . . Even if she looked like a Digger squaw it wouldn't matter to most of them. Cushman watched the miners thoughtfully.

"I'll be all right, Mr. Cushman. Don't fret yourself." Miss Drago gave him an amused smile.

Cushman shot her a sharp look. Wherever she came from, no matter what her background was, she had been around. She had read his thoughts and that was unusual, for he generally did not care enough about what happened to anyone to allow worry for others to show in his expression.

She walked away unhurriedly, thrusting her hands into the deep pockets of her white jacket. There was a faint blueness gathering on the high snow masses of the mountains. The sun was gone and cold was gathering in the basin.

Dunbar came trotting up. "How about giving me a hand with the skinning, huh? I've got two others to help. I want to get those hides off while they're still warm."

Cushman shook his head. "I'm going back to the river tonight."

"Why?"

Not often did anyone ask Cushman his business. He was surprised now that he did not resent Dunbar's question. "No feed for my horses."

"I had two sacks of hay under my bunk all winter. Figured to refill my mattress with it but I never got to it. I gave the sacks to the gal for her horse but she'll split with you, I know."

"Uh-uh."

"You don't like her?"

"That's got nothing to do with it, Dunbar."

"Just asked. If it's only the horses you're worried about, I'll see that they get fed. Wish you'd stay, Cushman. I'm worried about something else."

The two men stared at each other.

"They're a good bunch here in camp. Don't get me wrong," Dunbar said. "But maybe I'll need some help." He shook his head. "She ain't the kind you're thinking she is."

"No? Even if she ain't, why trust me?"

"You ain't been cooped up here all winter," Dunbar said simply.

There were a few men like Dunbar in every camp and town, Cushman thought—men who took responsibility. They started early talking about public buildings, tax levies, street drainage, fire protection. Generally they wound up owning the town. Dunbar was one of them. He was trying right now to organize a police force.

"I'll stay tonight," Cushman said. "Right now I want to take care of my horses."

"I'll help you, and then we can get to the skinning."

They went past a solid cabin with a lean-to built over a woodpile. "My place," Dunbar said. There were two huts with snow drifted high against the doors. Behind the next cabin Cushman saw a half of beef hanging in the trees. He noted the horse tracks near the place and the smoke coming from the chimney. This was where the woman was staying. "I own this one, too," Dunbar said. "Funny thing, she wouldn't stay there overnight without paying me." Dunbar seemed to take no offense from Miss Drago's insistence on paying her way.

Twenty yards farther on they came to a cabin where the snow lay to the eaves on one side. It was the last one up the main gulch, dirt-roofed and inhospitable-appearing. They unsaddled the horses and carried Cushman's gear inside. There was a small fireplace, a packing box cupboard, a pole bunk with spruce boughs for a mattress, a hewed plank table made from a single log, and a three-legged stool with a broken leg. Cushman could see daylight in a dozen places between the logs. All the cold of the mountain winter seemed to be concentrated inside.

They kicked some of the snow away on the lee side to make a place for the horses. Dunbar went to get the hay. Cushman heard him talking to Miss Drago, and then Dunbar crossed the irregular street to find Kenton. Presently he returned with a sack of hay.

Blue dusk was in the basin by the time they finished skinning the steers with the help of the two miners Dunbar had enlisted. Cushman's fingers were aching and the hides they had thrown aside were already frozen.

Dunbar said, "How about eating with me, Cushman?"

"No thanks."

"Well, let's go over to Big John's and have a few drinks, at least. I'll fix the deed up for you while we're there."

"No thanks," Cushman said again.

He walked back toward his cabin with a hind quarter of meat. One of the miners said to Dunbar, "He's an unsociable bastard, Jake. Does he figure on staying?"

"Help yourself to my wood or anything you need in the cabin," Dunbar called.

The Drago woman came to her doorway to throw out a pan of water as Cushman was passing with an armload of wood. She had to wait for him to go on. He caught a glimpse of the inside of the place, and it was no better than his. He wondered at the quality of ambition that would bring a woman to Victory even in the summer.

Heat drove the staleness from the cabin. Cushman cooked a meal at the fireplace and was eating it from the fry pan when Dunbar came in with a lamp.

"I don't like the way the talk is shaping up in Big John's place, Cushman. Before the evening is over somebody is going to try to prove what kind of woman she is."

"Sure."

"You're going to help me, ain't you?"

"She's got a bar on her door, Dunbar."

Dunbar's blue eyes were worried. "You haven't been here like a monk all winter. Maybe you don't realize how rough some of the boys can get when they're all likkered up."

"She knew that risk when she came here."

"Yeah. You going to help me or not?"

Cushman considered. "Let's say anyone she doesn't want in her cabin doesn't get in. Is that enough for you?"

"You put it in a left-hand way, Cushman. Sure, she served you a dirty trick when she beat you here with the cattle, but after all, she's a lone woman, and—"

"I said I'd give you a hand."

Dunbar gave Cushman a long look, and it struck Cushman that the man, in spite of his flustered air, was a tough customer. "All right, then." Dunbar went out. Bitter cold rushed in before he could close the door and with it came a burst of loud talk and laughter from the saloon.

After a time Cushman put on his coat and went out. His footsteps creaked on the snow and the bite of the air sent needles into his lungs. He had arrived half an hour late with his steers and he was at least six weeks early to work the claim he had traded them for. He was a damned fool to stay here, but one place was like another. Twenty years from now it would be some other forlorn place like this, or a lonely fire down a far trail that led nowhere.

Light was showing faintly against a blanket over the single window in the woman's cabin as he passed on his way to the saloon.

The first man Cushman noticed when he entered Big John's place was Joe Kenton. He was at the bar with three miners who seemed to be making much of him, and he was so drunk he could hardly stay upright.

CHAPTER EIGHT

Big John Freemantle's place was both store and saloon, the fireplace in the store part giving some warmth to that section of the room, and the bar at the other end supplying the heat there.

Kenton was drunk, but not too loaded to recognize Cushman. He gave Cushman a hostile, foggy stare as Cushman made himself a place at the bar. Big John rinsed a glass in a bucket of snow water and set out a drink. He was a huge, red-faced man with a mane of sandy hair like wind-blown straw. He wore a sweeping mustache that held its stiff sweep clear beyond his cheeks.

Jake Dunbar elbowed in beside Cushman. "I've got the deed." He seemed to be jovially drunk as he went with Cushman to a table near the fireplace. "They're making bets about the Drago woman. They're wondering—"

"Let's see the deed to that snowbank, Dunbar."

While Cushman was reading the paper Dunbar said, "Handy Grimes and Pete Eliot got Kenton drunk as a fiddler's bitch. He won't be any good to us." He was dead serious and not even close to being drunk.

Cushman glanced toward the bar and the young men full of health and whisky. Isolation and hard independence had made them a law unto themselves. They were a breed apart from the emigrants who took their families and moral values with them. Still, they were no worse than men Cushman had seen in other Western camps and towns.

"Get somebody to witness our signing," Cushman said.

A miner thumped a poke on the slab bar and shouted, "Fifteen ounces to back me up! She wouldn't have come here if she was a decent woman. Who wants to cover?"

"The dust, you mean?" somebody asked, and there was a bellow of laughter.

"It's Grimes and Eliot that I'm worried about most," Dunbar said, "but there's others too that—"

"I ain't sleeping in front of her door. Get a witness for this deed."

Dunbar brought over Big John and a miner named Mark Allen. They witnessed the deed and Allen said, "What's your guess about her, Big John?"

"You test whisky by drinking it," the saloonman said, and went back to the bar. Allen thought a moment, puzzled, and then he laughed and lurched away to tell the miners at the bar what Big John had said.

Cushman dropped a silver dollar on the table. "Will that cover the hay?"

Dunbar nodded. "I heard Kenton tell what happened at the river the other day. You're touchy, Cushman."

Cushman made no comment.

"You wouldn't take her money, but you want me to take yours."

Cushman stood up.

"You'll be awake?"

"I'll wake up if there's any need, Dunbar."

Under the cold stars Cushman went back to his cabin. There was no light showing in the window of the Drago woman's place. He checked his horses, huddled against each other beside the cabin wall. In the morning he would take them back to the valley and find a place to board them.

Big John Freemantle was the first to come to the woman's cabin. Lying awake, Cushman heard his heavy tread on the snow and then the sound of his voice as he knocked on the door and called out in a low voice, "Miss Drago, I would like to talk to you a few minutes."

He did not sound drunk or excited, and his accent was definitely that of an educated Englishman. Cushman raised on one elbow and peered through a gap in the logs. He could see Big John standing back from the doorway, immense in the starlight, a great, bushy fur cap on his head. The lights were still on in the saloon and the sound of merriment still came from there.

Apparently Miss Drago asked a question, for Big John gave his name. And then Cushman heard the scraping of her door as she opened it. She asked, "What is it, Mr. Freemantle?"

Big John took off his bushy cap. "I'm a man of some refinement, Miss Drago, although I daresay you've no cause to have observed that so far. I've some property here and I make a good living. I've money in a bank in Denver and some income from home. I neither smoke nor drink excessively and ordinarily I am not a violent man." Big John hesitated.

"Yes, Mr. Freemantle?"

"There's no need to make a long tale of it. I offer you marriage, Miss Drago."

If any woman had a right to inquire about the suddenness of a marriage proposal, Miss Drago certainly did. She must be standing with the door partly open, in the flow of the bitter cold, here in a God-forsaken gulch, looking at a man she had never seen until today. Cushman strained to hear her answer.

She said, "Why do you ask me, Mr. Freemantle?"

"I am not a man of impulse," Big John said. "My judgments are quick, as you can see, but generally well founded. I am attracted to you by your handsomeness and your courage. Then, too, it seems to me that a woman coming as you have alone to a place of men must be seeking a husband, or other compensations. As a husband I'm the best qualified man in this camp. Will you marry me?"

Cold poured against Cushman's nose and across his cheeks as he pressed against the crack.

"I'm flattered," the woman said, "but I did not come here to seek a husband. Good night."

"Wait," Big John said, not moving from where he stood. "It occurred to me that you could have found better-looking, wealthy men somewhere else." He turned his head toward the saloon for a moment. "Now I will speak of the other compensations. I have here one hundred dollars in gold. May I come in?"

"No," the woman said calmly. "Now you can go back and make your report to the rest of them."

"And be laughed at as a fool who was twice wrong? No, I will make no report. I came here for myself only."

Cushman heard the door close and a bar bang into place. Big John put on his cap and walked away. After he had gone some distance, Cushman heard him say,

"You can go back to bed, Dunbar, and I'll break you in two if you repeat anything you heard."

Big John was part gentleman and part roughneck. Cushman had no doubt that he meant every word which came from those two parts of his nature. Cushman snuggled back into his blankets. There had been simplicity in the scene and at the same time a large element of ludicrousness. For one of the few times in his life he had a genuine desire to laugh.

The tone of the sounds at the saloon was growing wilder. Some of the celebrators no doubt would be harmless before long, but there would be others beyond caring what they did before the night was over.

He was asleep when the group came up the street and stopped before the Drago woman's cabin. Their singing and their loud shouts woke him. They pounded on the door and asked her to come to the saloon with them for a drink.

"We'll drink and dance all night!"

Cushman couldn't hear what the woman said but he knew it was refusal. The three continued to hammer on the door and talk, and then one became obscene.

Dunbar called out, "That's enough, Eliot! You boys get away from there and go to bed."

"To hell with you, Dunbar! Just because we elected you mayor of this dump, ain't no reason for you—"

"Go on to bed," Dunbar said. "Leave her alone."

The three fell into a drunken argument. They were too far gone to know what they were doing. After a time they started to their cabins across the creek. One man fell over a sluice and the other two fell into the creek trying to help him. Cushman heard them cursing the cold and their injuries as they limped away.

There were four in the next group that came to the woman's cabin. They were trying to walk quietly, and that wakened Cushman more quickly than the sounds of the loudly drunken three. Two of them stopped at the door like prowling animals. The other two went around to the masked window, staggering as they walked.

The pair at the door grunted as they tried to push the barrier down. They backed up and tried again with a rush. Cushman slipped his boots on and stepped to the door. He heard Dunbar call out, "Get away from there!"

"Mind your own business, Jake!"

"Back away!" Dunbar called. "I'll shoot."

"We'll jam your pistol down your throat if you do!"

Cushman eased the door open and looked past the corner of the logs. The two men at the window, lurching in a snowdrift, were trying to wrench the window from its frame. One of the men before the door was rubbing his shoulder. "There must be a double bar across the damn thing."

"Give me a knife and I'll cut the hinges."

Dunbar was standing down the street. "Cushman!"

"Here," Cushman said. To the intruders he called, "Get away from there."

"That snooty new bastard," one of the men said. He had a knife in his hand and was kneeling, trying to probe along the door jamb to find the leather hinges. For a moment all four men at the woman's cabin were silent.

Inside, Miss Drago cried, "I'm armed. I warn you!"

"Looks like everybody's heeled," a man muttered.

The backbone of it seemed to be broken. Then a long tongue of flame leaped from a pistol in the street. Cushman heard the bullet strike the logs of his cabin. The horses jumped. The man shot at Cushman again. From inside the woman's cabin came the muffled explosion of a light pistol. The two miners at the window stumbled back to their companions.

Dunbar fired two shots. Leaping to the shadows at the corner of his cabin, Cushman knew by the lancing of the muzzle blasts that Dunbar was firing high. Coldly angry, Cushman sighted on the group of miners. At the last instant he raised his rifle and fired above their heads, but he thought he was a fool to do so because one of them had tried to kill him.

They broke and ran as he was working the Henry for another shot. Like a pack of fleeing wolves they fled across the snow, scattering toward the excited shouts coming from the huts and cabins of Victory.

Dunbar came running up the street. He was fully dressed, Cushman observed. He stopped at the woman's cabin and called out, "Dunbar! Are you all right in there, miss?" Cushman heard the door scrape open and the woman said, "I'm quite all right, thank you, Mr. Dunbar." She was as calm as if Dunbar had asked her if he could borrow flour.

Acutely conscious of the cold, now that the excitement was over, Cushman went back into his cabin. He had no wish to talk to any of the miners who were running up the gulch, shouting questions. In a moment Dunbar knocked on the door. "Cushman, are you all right?"

"I'm going to bed."

Dunbar pushed in. He was breathing hard. "You didn't hit any of them, did you?"

"No."

"They were all drunk, you know. They—"

"They were drunk," Cushman said. As far as he was concerned, a man was responsible for his actions at all times. "Go quiet the rest of the fools and leave me alone."

"Sure," Dunbar said quietly. "But they're not fools, not the way you make the word come out." He went out and Cushman heard him talking to the men in the street.

After another hour Victory settled down to frozen stillness. Before he went to sleep Cushman considered the fact that the Drago woman must have shot only to scare the miners trying to break into her cabin; she could not have missed if she had fired directly into the door or window.

She had learned some basic facts about men the hard way. Tomorrow they would laugh about their repulse and some of them would apologize to her, but if she had killed one of them . . . A woman had no right to kill a man who held himself not responsible for his acts because of drunkenness.

CHAPTER NINE

Daylight was seeping through the cracks in the logs when Dunbar came into Cushman's cabin. He entered without knocking, an assumption that he was welcome. Ordinarily Cushman would have been angry with any man who did so, but there was a cheerfulness in Dunbar and an air of honest eagerness about him that overrode Cushman's surly feelings.

"Get to moving," Dunbar said. "She's invited us to breakfast."

Cushman swung out of his bunk and looked sourly at the dead fireplace and the frying pan with ashes blown into the grease of last night's cooking. "She wants to pay us for what we did last night, huh?"

"Sure." Dunbar paused. "You got paying on the brain, ain't you? Another thing, she knows we'll advertise her cooking, if it's any good, so when she gets that wagon here everybody will be hammering a plate and licking their chops. That woman has got a head for getting along."

"Yeah, she sure as hell has."

"I don't blame you for being a little sore about the oxen. It was business, of course—" Dunbar stopped and regarded Cushman thoughtfully. "You ain't sore, after all, are you?"

"No." Cushman began to dress.

"Hm." Dunbar changed the subject. "Did you know any of those four last night? Recognize 'em, I mean?"

"No. Did you?"

"Sure," Dunbar said. "All of them. They were just drunk and wild, Cushman. Drunkenness made them go directly at something that every man in camp would like to try, including you and me. Ain't that right?"

Cushman smiled faintly. "That's right."

"You heard Big John last night?" Dunbar asked.

Cushman nodded.

"He's got a hell of a pride about some things, Big John has." Dunbar fished around for words. "I'd suggest—"

"Let's say I never heard him."

"Good! That's what I was trying to get at. Come on. You can wash up at my shack and then we'll go sample her grub." Dunbar laughed suddenly. "That Big John, standing there like a bear, making a fine speech . . ."

Cushman was mildly surprised to see Big John ahead of them when he and Dunbar went to Miss Drago's cabin. Big John was sitting straight-backed on a stool. He appeared to be at ease, although he gave Cushman and Dunbar long, slow scrutiny when he spoke to them.

Although she had gone through a night which had been enough to give most women the megrims, Miss Drago was quite composed. Her long-sleeved shirtwaist with trim white cuffs made a startling contrast against the crudity of the cabin. "I'm afraid you gentlemen will have to sit on the bed." She took their hats with a quiet smile.

Big John's sandy hair had been beaten down with water. His shirt was clean but badly wrinkled, and the dark red cravat he was wearing looked as if it had just been taken from long storage in a sack. He said, "How early were you awake last night, Cushman?"

How much did you hear of what I said, Cushman?

Miss Drago was stooping to lift the lid of a Dutch oven on the hearth. She waited for the answer. Dunbar fidgeted on the bed beside Cushman, as if he would like to do the answering himself, not trusting Cushman.

"Let's say I was awake some time after you went back to the saloon," Cushman said.

Big John found the answer acceptable. He smiled and a minor crisis was over, but his expression was still reserved and thoughtful whenever he looked directly at Cushman.

Cushman ate automatically and was halfway through breakfast before it occurred to him that the food was very good. He watched Miss Drago's hands as she poured coffee. They were long-fingered, strong hands and they showed the marks of weather and work. Obviously, she was not too recently removed from the life of a lady.

She explained about the restaurant she was going to establish. For a time at least it would be run from the wagon. If business warranted she would erect a building later. In either case the operation would be on a cash-and-carry basis. Those who wanted to eat would bring their own utensils, be served, and take their food away to eat where they pleased.

Big John and Dunbar approved of the plan.

"You'll do well," Big John said. "When the weather breaks we'll have two hundred men here, I don't doubt."

"How about supplies?" Dunbar asked.

"I've arranged with Mr. Kenton's brothers to freight them in from Denver as often as needed."

Dunbar glanced at Cushman. "I hope Kenton's brothers are better drivers than he is."

Belle Drago colored slightly. "It was my fault that my wagon got stuck in the river. I was driving. Mr. Kenton was riding ahead to show me the way, but I used my own judgment."

So she was not quite the self-sufficient Amazon she had pretended to be. She was a woman who had invaded the province of men. Now she had made a small admission of the fact, and it helped Cushman to understand her a little better.

But still he did not understand her very well. She was no whore, that was certain, but where had she gained the experience to move so easily in a man's world? Cushman asked a question almost before he realized that he was going to do so.

"Have you got any brothers, Miss Drago?"

The woman gave him a quick look. "No. Why did you ask?" She was disturbed and on the defensive.

"I just wondered."

Miss Drago kept studying Cushman. "Wasn't that an odd question?"

"It just occurred to me." Cushman was uncomfortable. He resented Big John's heavy stare. Once more Dunbar was fidgeting. They both were intelligent men and Cushman knew that they understood exactly why he had asked the question.

He met Big John's hostile look and sent back his own challenge. There was a bold streak of arrogance in Big John. It thrust out and dueled with the bitterly independent quality of Cushman's make-up. When they looked away from each other, their antagonism was subtly, deeply set.

Dunbar missed nothing. He said, "You'll be needing some help with the wagon, Miss Belle."

"I think not, thank you, Mr. Dunbar. More coffee?"

After breakfast the three men stood in the street for a few moments. The camp looked utterly dead. A sharp cold still glittered in the basin, although the sun was touching it. Sluice boxes shone with frost and ice made blue-white veins of the small ditches leading to the sluices.

Dunbar sniffed the air eagerly and said, "Spring is on its way."

Big John adjusted his fur cap. "I've decided she's a lady, Cushman. *You* haven't made up your mind. Be careful when you do." He walked away, jumping the ice-edged creek with a light bound.

Once more Dunbar let words flow in to cover the tingling gap. "Will you be taking your horses down at the same time Miss Belle and Kenton—"

Watching Big John, Cushman said, "You mean am I going to let Kenton ride back, instead of walk?"

"That's exactly what I was getting at."

"Where'd you get such a big social conscience?" That was one of Billy Bodega's favorite expressions.

It fell cheap and flat against Dunbar's quiet expression. "What gave you the chip on the shoulder about lifting a hand to help anybody, Cushman?"

Dunbar's way of striking so deeply inside Cushman was disturbing. The direct honesty of him made it difficult for Cushman to take offense but he did not feel obliged to give answers about his personal life to Dunbar or any other man.

"How'd you know her name was Belle?" Cushman asked.

"I asked her."

Cushman went to get his ax to chop up his steer. Dunbar started whacking up the others. When Cushman had finished, he hesitated for a time and then he went over and began to help Dunbar.

They were working together on the last steer when Kenton came from the saloon. His gait was curiously sidling, but he was no longer drunk. Stubborn, brutish anger was smeared across his expression as he asked, "Who tried to get in her cabin?"

Dunbar shook his head.

Kenton turned reddened, cloudy eyes on Cushman, who did not bother to shake his head.

"Cute, the two of you, ain't you?" Kenton said. "Was you in on it?"

"No," Dunbar said, "and if you want a cracked head ask that question again." He was as tough and sure of himself as he was quiet. "Why don't you go ask Miss Belle?"

Kenton picked up the severed front leg of one of the steers. He marched toward the nearest cabin. He burst through the doorway and demanded to know where Grimes and Eliot lived.

The inmates resented being roused by a red-eyed maniac with a steer leg in his hand. One of them shouted, "Get the hell out of here!" There were more words, curses, and then the thump of a heavy blow. "They're in the first cabin this side of the saloon!"

Kenton rushed out. A miner with his hair on end, holding his shoulder, staggered into the doorway and took a wild look around the camp. He saw Cushman and Dunbar standing with their axes by the steer carcasses. Kenton was charging toward Eliot's cabin, his left shoulder lowered and thrust ahead, the war club swinging.

Hangover-addled and still shocked by his rude awakening, the miner in the doorway said, "By Ned, that bear has got a sore nose!"

Kenton went into Eliot's cabin with a bang. In a moment there were shouts and curses and a great threshing about and a clatter of tinware. It was over quickly. Kenton roared, "That'll show you!" He emerged with the steer leg in his hand, rolling his head like a grizzly as he looked around the camp. He tossed the weapon into a snowbank and went toward Miss Drago's cabin.

Dunbar went running to see what had happened. Big John came out of the saloon and two miners followed him. Cushman stayed where he was. Kenton had clubbed two of the less guilty from last night's trouble, but it would do.

Cushman began to carry meat to the snowbank behind his cabin. He had made several trips before Dunbar came back.

"He like to hammered those two to death," Dunbar said. "He almost tore Orley Baker's ear off with that hoof in the first cabin, and then he fixed Eliot and Grimes up real good with broken ribs and noses and assorted lumps." He grinned.

Dunbar dug a rude sled out of the snow behind his cabin. They dragged it with Cushman's pack horse and stored all the meat in the snow. "Comes a quick thaw and I'll wonder why I ever made this deal," Dunbar said. "What do I owe you?"

"Nothing."

Dunbar took a silver dollar from his pocket. There was humor in his eyes but behind that was a deep understanding. "This is the buck you gave me for the hay." He held it out, and Cushman took it.

There was something of Jeremy Flint in Dunbar and something also of Sam Hildreth and Billy Bodega, all men whom Cushman had liked without ever expressing his feelings. He put the dollar away. He would never make that mistake again with Jake Dunbar.

They went to Dunbar's cabin for a pot of coffee.

"Now tell me the facts about my claim," Cushman said.

"Just what I said. I gave three hundred for it myself. The man who owned it went back east before he did anything more than build a sluice. It may be a good claim, it may be a stinker. I thought it was worth a chance."

"How's the gulch in general?"

"Fair," Dunbar said. "I imagine there's a hundred thousand dollars in dust laying under bunks and stuck away in cupboards in Victory, not counting what Big John has taken in. When everybody comes back, we'll probably clean the gulch out in a summer, but that's the way it goes. California Gulch is done. Cache Creek is playing out—no placer camp lasts long. You get your gold while it's there and then you go home or move on to the next workings."

"Which are you going to do?" Cushman asked.

Dunbar walked over to his bunk and stripped back the ragged blankets and the hay-filled mattress. He used both hands to lift a buckskin bag. It thumped heavily when he put it on the table before Cushman. Dunbar untied the strings and spread the wheel of leather. The mass revealed looked like a pile of dull copper filings at first, but as the finer particles slid down the mound, shining faintly as they spilled away, coursing around nuggets as large as the end of a man's little finger, Cushman knew that he was looking upon the largest amount of gold he had ever seen.

He guessed there was about ten thousand dollars' worth. He picked up a nugget and scratched at it with his thumbnail and tossed it back and watched the dully shining grains stream away in a miniature landslide.

"Your winter's work?" he asked.

"Most of it. Some from late last summer after I added four sections to my sluice." Dunbar watched Cushman intently. "It's generally not a good idea to show a man that much gold at once."

"No."

"I carry a poke with about a hundred bucks in it, like everyone else. You're the first man I ever showed the whole pile to."

Cushman gave the miner an inquiring look.

"You don't much give a damn for anything, do you, Cushman? I noticed it before in the way you got rid of those steers. Most men would have been sore as hell, but you just dropped the whole thing as if it didn't matter. At first I figured you had a poker face, but now I know better. You just don't care."

"That's it."

Dunbar pulled the puckered edges of the buckskin wheel together, retied the thong, and put the gold away. He put one foot on a stool and stared seriously at Cushman. "That gold didn't arouse half as much interest in you as those biscuits did this morning."

"You can eat biscuits."

"What *do* you want, Cushman?"

"Who the hell are you to ask me?"

Dunbar shrugged. "It was just a question, that's all. I suppose a man judges everyone else by himself. We want something, or think we do. When I came back to Illinois from the war, I thought I wanted a butcher shop. The easy way to get it was to come out here, scoop up a few pocketfuls of gold, and then go home and buy my shop. Five thousand was what I aimed for. Now I've got the five thousand, but I don't want the butcher shop." Dunbar shook his head.

Cushman said, "You've got one out in the snow."

Dunbar smiled, but there was puzzled ruefulness in the expression. "I needed those steers like I need a white shirt. All the time I was so hot on getting them I couldn't figure why, but now I know. I put in four years of my life thinking I wanted a butcher shop, telling myself that was why I was out here.

"Finally I must have realized I was never going back home, but I'd lived so close to the idea all the time that I had to do something about it. I bought the steers and that's my butcher shop. Now I'm free of the idea." Dunbar peered sharply at Cushman. "Does that sound crazy?"

"No. What *do* you want, Dunbar?"

"I want enough money to start lode mining when it begins to develop. It will, too, before long." Dunbar flung his hand toward the bed where his gold was. "That and all the rest that's been washed out pinch by pinch is only a dribble compared to the gold that's in these hills somewhere. It took centuries for a few handfuls of gold to be washed down from somewhere up there."

Dunbar pointed toward the mountains and Cushman visualized them standing there just beyond the cabin, tremendous and snow-clad.

"Here, or at the head of some other gulch, some day I'll find where gold-bearing rock is in place. I want to mine it right where it took millions of years to form. I'll build a smelter that'll belch smoke day and night. I'll have a railroad to it, and there'll be a town. I'll have five hundred men tearing into that mountain, ripping ore out and spilling it down to my smelter. I'll have—" Dunbar stopped suddenly, realizing how far he had flown from the draughty, dirt-floored cabin.

He went to the hearth and lifted the coffee pot. He shook it, estimated the amount of grounds inside against the amount of liquid. There was enough coffee for half a cup more for each of them. When it was poured Dunbar sat down on the stool. "And I'll have a special fund to keep coffee in the house all the time, so I won't have to use the same grounds for weeks at a time." His honest grin flashed out. "Do you reckon I've been out in the mountains too long?"

"No," Cushman said. Dunbar had his feet on the ground and knew what he was doing. His dream was honest, and it was bigger than the dreams that most men hold. He didn't want riches, or he would have talked of riches, of the things that gold could buy, of the power it gave to its owner. Dunbar wanted action, accomplishment; he wished to create things from his vision and work.

It was that side of the picture, rather than the dream itself, that impressed Cushman and lifted him for a time from his careful, narrow way of thinking. Dunbar's enthusiasm and energy were greater forces than the mere vision of a golden mountain. Although he was dreamless himself, Cushman felt the fire of another's ambition, and it left him with the haunted thought that he had been traveling savagely toward nowhere ever since he rode away with Jeremy Flint from Ruby Valley twelve years ago.

Dunbar finished his coffee and brushed the cup aside with a flip of his hand. "Now that you're a claim owner, you'll figure on staying the summer?"

"I'll have to," Cushman said. "I've got to get the price of my steers out of that ground."

"I can sell it for you. I'll even buy it back myself. You're not interested in gold, Cushman."

Cushman heard a horse going by in the street, and a few moments later he heard the Drago woman and Kenton talking. "I'll stay a while, Dunbar," he said. He rose from the table. "Right now I've got to take my horses to the valley."

Belle Drago and Kenton were preparing to leave when

Cushman passed the woman's cabin. Kenton was rigging a rope stirrup. Cushman glanced at Miss Drago's long skirts and thought, Of course she's got to ride sidesaddle. It must have been miserably awkward for her going through the tight timber on the way here.

Cushman said, "I'm going down. If Kenton cares to ride my pack horse, he's welcome."

The woman looked Cushman over carefully. "Thank you," she said.

"I'll be ready in a minute." Over his shoulder Cushman called back, "I'm going the long way."

When he was ready to go Cushman went to his meat cache in the snowbank and dug into it. He started to take a front shoulder, and then some compulsion made him shove it back into the snow. He took a haunch instead, wrapping it in canvas and tying it behind the saddle, before he joined Kenton and the woman.

They went down the broad gulch in the rising warmth of late morning. The sun glare striking from the peaks was blinding, and through it Cushman saw the faint discoloration of thaw up high. Before they reached the lower end of the gulch they were riding in thin mud. Unconsciously, Cushman scouted a wagon route. A few more days of warm weather and Campanero Creek would be booming and the crossings a wagon would have to make would be difficult.

On the mesa above the prospector's cabin Cushman said, "I'll meet you later." He didn't wait for an answer before he sent his horse sliding down the steep gravel bank.

The Arkansas was rising. Brown water was lapping at the prospector's gravel bar, threatening to go over it soon. The man himself was standing on the bank watching the stream eagerly. Because of the water he did not hear Cushman until Cushman was quite close. Then the prospector swung around quickly. His face went sour. "Oh! You again."

Cushman untied the meat, unwrapped it and gave it to the prospector without dismounting. The man stared at it a moment and then pointed to the river. "She's starting the runoff! Before it's over my bar will be two feet higher and loaded with heavy gold!"

"Or washed away," Cushman said. "They did pretty well up at Victory all winter. You could get set there, maybe, before everybody—"

"I'm not moving! The river's rising, and I'll be here when she goes down!"

Cushman tied the bloody canvas behind the saddle and rode away. Meat, not advice, was about what every man wanted. Even those who asked for advice didn't want it unless it agreed with what they had in mind already. He looked back before he started up the bank.

The prospector was running toward his cabin, carrying the haunch of beef in both hands against his chest.

The poor bastard, Cushman thought. But no one had forced the man to wolf out the winter there on the rocky Arkansas.

When Cushman again met Belle Drago and Kenton, they both looked at the canvas behind his saddle and made no comment. For a time all three of them rode in silence and then Cushman said, "There's a fellow mining down there. He was short of meat."

Again, neither the woman nor Kenton said anything, but they glanced at each other as if passing private information, and Cushman's irritation increased. He said, "I don't suppose, Miss Drago, that you can understand what it is to go without food."

She gave him a startled look. In the instant before she looked away, he saw a curious expression of pain in her eyes, almost as if she pitied him. "There are worse things, perhaps, Mr. Cushman."

Kenton asked, "What part of the country are you from, Cushman?"

From where, indeed? Cushman asked himself. Illinois was far lost, with only sentimental boyish memories of it troubling him now and then. It seemed that he had grown up in Ruby Valley, but he knew that wasn't so. Should he speak like old Sko-kup's medicine man, of an origin from rocks and fire and arid earth and desert sunsets? At least the Indians had answers to such questions, vague and unsatisfactory though they were to white men.

Cushman pointed westward and let it serve. Belle Drago watched him keenly and took the answer, but Kenton persisted stubbornly. "From California, you mean?"

"I've never been to California and never will be," Cush-

man said curtly. He rode on ahead, away from the
woman's steady appraisal of him.

They came to the wagon in the grove. The cases of
food were still piled on the ground where Cushman had
first seen them. Once she had got the wagon from the
river, Belle Drago hadn't wasted a second beating him to
Victory, Cushman thought. He looked out at the river. It
was running hard above the big rocks. A man would have
a bad time trying to hold his feet out there now.

Cushman looked inside the wagon. The side boards
were extraordinarily high and all along them were tightly
built cupboards, tables that let down on hinges, and cooking utensils tied down on racks. The stove was bedded
in four buckets of sand bolted to the floor. A sailor's hammock was slung on gripes across the wagon.

Belle Drago was giving Kenton instructions. "I'll load
the wagon while you go to a ranch and arrange for horses
and a driver to take us on to Victory."

Cushman said, "I can do that. I've got to go to one
of the ranches anyway."

"He could, maybe," Kenton said. "That way I can stay
here and load the wagon. It ain't no work for you, Miss
Drago."

"Never mind what's work for me." Belle Drago looked
at Cushman. "You wouldn't mind doing that?"

"I've got to go to one of the ranches anyway."

"Would you— Would it be too much trouble for you
to take my horse along and leave him there with the
others?"

It struck Cushman that Belle Drago was defensive and
embarrassed when she asked the question. She was like a
child who expects refusal. "I'll take him along," Cushman said. As he rode away he wondered about the hesitan-
cy in the woman's simple request of a favor that a man
would have taken for granted.

She had a strange, high pride, but it was not, after all,
imperiousness. She had actually been afraid and ashamed
to ask for help; and her fear of refusal had come from
something more basic than the fact that she had bested
Cushman in the matter of the steers.

At the first ranch Cushman made arrangements with
the owner to keep the horses until the grass was up in the
high country. The rancher had a team of six blue mules.

He was proud of them. For twenty dollars he said he would use them to take the wagon into Victory. "I guess you know that there's never been a wagon up there."

Cushman declined the rancher's invitation to stay the night. The rancher would talk his head off. Cushman walked back to the camp on the river. The wagon was already packed and ready to be moved. "A man will be here tomorrow."

He sat on a log eating food that Belle Drago served him. "May as well go on back with you tomorrow."

Across the fire Kenton stirred a little and stared darkly at Cushman. Firelight played across the woman's face. The river made a heavy rushing noise in the background. "I'll insist on paying you, Mr. Cushman."

Cushman acknowledged the woman's independent spirit. "I'll take it out in meals."

Before she retired, Belle Drago brought two blankets to Cushman. He heard the creaking of the hammock gripes when she went to bed. Kenton stirred the fire and looked steadily at Cushman. In a low voice Kenton said, "I'll be keeping one eye on you, mister."

In the man's dark gaze Cushman read more than loyalty to Belle Drago. Kenton was in love with her. Before long, half the men in Victory would think they were too.

There was a faint, elusive odor to the blankets Belle Drago had given Cushman. The scent disturbed him.

At sunrise the rancher arrived with the mules, their harness rattling as they came through the grove. They were all raw, wild power and stubbornness for a while after they started up the bank with the wagon.

It took two hard days to reach the camp. Cushman and Kenton chopped trees, made crossings on Campanero Creek, levered rocks out of the way, and snubbed the top-heavy wagon with ropes around trees to keep it from tipping over on sidling grades.

During the last half-mile most of the population of Victory came down to help. When the big mules hauled the wagon to a level place near Belle Drago's cabin, she stood up in the seat and said, "The first meal will be served in two hours. Bring your own fighting tools and one dollar and a half."

Largely veterans of the Civil War, the miners roared at

the familiar term "fighting tools" for knife and fork and spoon.

Kenton was already chopping wood for the stove.

Jake Dunbar gave Cushman a grave look. "Enjoy the trip?"

"I had to go to the valley anyway."

"Sure you did."

Cushman went up the street to his cabin. He observed that the snow had settled some since he had been gone. Up on the mountains the yellow glaze was growing on the great snowfields. The nights would be bitter for a long time yet but summer was not far off.

In front of his cabin, Cushman looked back at the crowd of miners milling around the wagon. Women were not sacred in the West because they were women; the law of supply and demand gave them high value which was often confused with other values. For simplicity's sake there were two classes: good and bad. But all men were inclined to seek proof of something bad in good women and something good in the other kind.

The testing was only started for Belle Drago.

CHAPTER TEN

As the snow tumbled away with the booming rush of Campanero Creek, men came hurrying into Victory. Some of them owned claims and were coming back after wintering elsewhere. Some of them owned little and were very anxious to acquire a great deal quickly.

Drawn together by their tenure in the camp, Jake Dunbar and others tried to keep mining law intact, but in spite of their efforts there was pre-emption of claims unattended and increasing trouble from the have-nots, until at last the veterans were forced to confine their efforts largely to taking care of themselves.

Cushman stood apart in all the disputes. He had his claim. He worked it. Let the others growl and squabble as they pleased. Let Dunbar fret and stew about everyday violation of mining law.

And then one day Cushman found himself in trouble.

Early in the morning he surprised two men making a cleanup at his sluice. He shot one in the shoulder as the man started to fire at him. When the second thief ran Cushman knocked his leg from under him with another shot. His action was direct, unthinking, fitting the just needs of the moment.

Before he knew it he was surrounded by friends of the two wounded men, and by men who imagined they were friends of the culprits. Jake Dunbar led a hard wedge of the veterans through the clamor. With drawn pistols and ready shotguns they established the truth of the affair, and gave the two groaning thieves till nightfall to get out of the gulch. Thus the determined action of a few was accepted as temporary law, not because there was justice on the side of the few but because there was united force.

Thereafter, no one tried to make a cleanup at Cushman's sluice, but one quick act had not brought order; thieves merely shifted operations to softer spots. Men now buried their gold beneath their cabin floors, and worked their sluices with one eye on their cabins—and a rifle handy.

Dunbar summed it up, "At first, you could hang your watch on your cabin door and be sure no one would touch it. Now you can't be sure the door will be there when you come back at night. It's always the way of these camps."

Belle Drago lived through it all with outward serenity. During her first month in camp she served meals from the wagon, and then, with the coming of lumber, she and Kenton built beside her cabin a building that was known at the Restaurant, although in the proper sense it was not that at all, but no more than a kitchen. Near the front door was a long serving window with a wide shelf, on which set an iron pot that served as a till. Diners presented their plates at the window. Wearing a white apron that was incongruous against his heavy boots and black beard, Kenton carried the plates to Miss Drago to be filled and then returned them to the window, watching sharply to be sure the proper amount of dust or coin went into the iron pot.

His was not a man's job, and Kenton suffered because of that. Each time a new group of arrivals saw him, they jeered and made insulting remarks. Kenton never forgot an insult or let one go unanswered. After supper he always hunted up his tormentors, selecting one as an example. And then he piled into him with such straight-out savagery that he became known as a man to avoid. One day at the serving window a miner underestimated Kenton's shrewdness on the basis of his stupid face and dropped pinches of iron pyrites into the till. On the sixth pinch, when the man was sure he had succeeded in getting a free meal, Kenton reached through the window, seized his arm, slammed it against the side of the window and broke it at the elbow.

Kenton had chosen himself a hard job for a healthy man in a new country. He could have quit it any time, but he chose to stay with his menial tasks. Belle Drago owned a claim on the creek above Cushman's, allowed her during her first week in camp after a solemn, four-hour meeting of all the miners to pass on the validity of her claim, as a woman, to being a citizen of Victory. She offered to lease the ground to Kenton on shares.

He said, "I'd rather stay here and work for you."

After regular hours at the restaurant, Big John, Dunbar and Cushman were often there. Joe Kenton always stayed until the last one left. He never missed any of their conversation and in unguarded moments they saw him giving them bitter, frustrated looks.

There could be little formality, and there was certainly no privacy, in the attention of the three men to Belle Drago.

She was always busy, baking bread for the next day's serving, making pies, checking the list of supplies for the next trip of the Kenton brothers. Her day began at four in the morning.

Big John and Dunbar and Cushman soon knew that they were trying to compete with a flourishing business. They seldom stayed longer than an hour, Dunbar and Big John talking while Belle Drago went on with her work. Cushman was the silent one.

One night Dunbar asked him, "Why do you go there, Cushman? All you do is sit and listen."

"That's all I generally ever do."

"She'd run us out if she didn't want us around, huh?"

"I reckon," Cushman said.

The three were not the only ones who paid attention to Belle Drago, although they were the only ones who were privileged to enter the restaurant after the boards were put over the serving window.

Bold men found ways to discover for themselves whether they were facing a matter of principle or price when Belle Drago declined all offers, including marriage. They ran their tests the best way they could, and then often did not know if the results were positive or not.

Russian Bob, who had built a saloon astraddle the creek, was of the opinion that Belle Drago was merely waiting for the highest bidder. He saw things with a gambler's eyes.

That she knew all the speculation and crosscurrents of opinion about her, Cushman did not doubt. She worked the best part of sixteen hours a day and seldom went beyond the restaurant or her cabin, but still she must have a fair idea of what men were saying about her.

Kenton's last chore of the evening was to carry three pails of water to the doorway of her cabin. Belle Drago bathed. No one was entirely opposed to a woman's right to bathe daily, but it was still a puzzling thing, like using high-toned language when there was no real need to do so.

In spite of himself Cushman was drawn into personal speculation about Belle Drago. One morning he strayed away from his claim at ten o'clock and went down to see if she would give him a cup of coffee.

Kenton was chopping wood. He paused in his work to give Cushman a sullen stare. At the serving window Cushman looked inside and saw Belle Drago washing clothes in a tub set on two benches. He felt guilty at the thought of disturbing her work and he was about to go away when she said, "Yes, Mr. Cushman?"

The "mister" was part of a barrier she put between herself and every man in camp, excepting Dunbar, whom she called by his first name.

"Nothing," Cushman said. He started to turn away.

"You wanted something or you wouldn't have stopped."

"A cup of coffee, but—"

"Come in then."

"Don't want to disturb you."

"You'll cause me a lot more disturbance by standing at that window where everyone can see I'm serving coffee between meals. Come inside."

Cushman went around to the door. The room was steamy with Belle Drago's washing and vapors from kettles on the stove. Cushman stood beside a worktable with his hat in his hands.

"Sit down, Mr. Cushman." The woman dried her rounded brown arms on a towel and poured two cups of coffee. She sat down across from Cushman. "I generally drink a cup of coffee in the middle of the morning." She should be tired out from constant work, but she did not look weary.

"How's the claim going?" she asked.

"All right, I guess." She was an attractive woman, Cushman thought. If she ever relaxed a little, lost some of her drive and determination, she could very well be a beautiful woman.

"There's three hundred men in camp now, Jake Dunbar says. He keeps track of such things." The woman glanced toward the serving window as an uproar that sounded like a fight broke out in the direction of Russian Bob's.

"Quite a few men, all right," Cushman said. He gave the woman a quick study while she was looking toward the window. Some carelessness in her appearance would have been allowable, for the country forced carelessness on everyone in some degree, but she was always neatly dressed and shining clean. Every few days her shirtwaists and skirts billowed on a clothesline between her cabin and a tree. She saw to it, too, that Kenton wore a clean apron every day, and that the restaurant was scrubbed clean every night.

When she turned her head from the window her eyes met Cushman's and they looked directly at each other for a time. "Where will you go from here?" she asked.

Cushman was startled but he hid his feelings and said, "I don't know."

"You *have* wandered around the country a good deal, haven't you?"

"I suppose."

"Why?"

It was a question that Cushman did not care to answer, nor was he sure he could if he had tried.

"Why, Mr. Cushman?"

Belle Drago's insistence was interrupted by a knock at the door. Big John called, "May I come in?"

He was a smooth, confident man, Big John. He made no pretense of being surprised at seeing Cushman sitting at a table with Belle Drago in the middle of the morning. He was civil enough in his greeting but Cushman felt the man's dislike of him, and he felt inside himself the subtle, primordial bristling of his own hostility toward Big John.

"This is the first time I've ever seen you here at this time of day, Cushman," Big John said.

"And it's the first time you've ever been here during working hours," Belle Drago said. "Sit down, Mr. Freemantle, and I'll get you some coffee."

Cushman decided that he would stay as long as Big John stayed. It would not be much of a contest because when Belle Drago resumed her work she would run them both out.

Big John's grin flashed under his sandy mustache. "You're half a century ahead of your time, Belle, and since you're a woman, you're doubly in error."

She poured the saloonman coffee. "What do you mean by that?"

"You've crossed the proper boundaries of womanly behavior without going all the way. No unmarried woman is supposed to invade a mining camp with a respectable business."

"I know. But it would be all right for me to drudge here if I were married to a husband that chased around the mountains looking for gold. He could come home when he was hungry. I could bear him another child and everything would be respectable."

"Perfectly." Big John laughed. "You know what I think? I think you know what you're doing. You came here to make money. You cheat no one, favor no one, and serve everybody better meals than some of these renegades were accustomed to getting at home, if they had homes. I give you credit and speculate no further."

If they had homes . . . Cushman gave Big John a hard glance. The man had an Englishman's arrogance and air of superiority, and maybe he was trying to get personal. But the saloonman was paying no attention to Cushman. He was talking easily to Belle Drago and she seemed to find his conversation interesting.

The woman said, "What's your opinion on the subject of me, Mr. Cushman?"

"Got none," Cushman said. Let Big John be the orator; he was better fitted for it.

"You puzzle the whole camp, Belle," Big John said. "As a dancehall woman or a madam, you could become a legend. In years to come men would tell pretty lies about you. Your beauty would grow beyond description, your kindness to the afflicted would multiply a thousand times, and men would invent some great, sad mystery to explain your past."

Cushman saw a sudden freezing in the woman's expression, but it flowed away quickly and she gave Big John an amused smile. "You're quite a speech-maker, Mr. Freemantle."

"I'm just a shopkeeper, with a shopkeeper's estimate of other people. I made my own bad guesses about you, Belle, and then I realized that you were an enterprising woman with courage enough to do something that few women would attempt. It's a shame, of course, that such beauty should be wasted in a place like this."

The woman smiled. "Go back to your shop, both of you. I have a washing to finish and dinner for a hundred men to get ready."

Kenton came in the back door. He was scowling as he dumped an armload of wood into the box beside the stove.

Going out, Cushman glanced back from the doorway. He saw Belle Drago watching him with a puzzled, troubled look, and then she attacked the washing again. In the street Big John stopped to light a cigar. "That Kenton," he said; "the dolt is in love with her. She ought to sack him and get some youngster to do his work."

"You followed me in there," Cushman said.

"Of course I did. You don't think I'm a man to stand idle and give another the advantage, do you?"

"What advantage?"

"Good Lord, Cushman, don't act stupid. I'll do my best to see that you don't have a chance to be alone with her. 'What advantage?'" Big John laughed. He went across the street toward his saloon.

Cushman walked back to his claim. One of his dark moments flashed across his mind. He remembered watching Beth Clendenin wave to him through the dust of wagons pulling out of Ruby Valley. He wondered if she had married the tall Kentuckian.

CHAPTER ELEVEN

Working at his sluice one afternoon, Cushman was debating with himself about going to the valley for his horses. The grass was high enough now in the high country around Victory to support the animals. Cushman knew he had no real need for the horses and that they were better off where they were, but he kept wondering about going after them until he recognized the truth: aimlessness was driving him again, the feeling that he should move on and seek something over the mountains.

Jake Dunbar came by towing a pack horse loaded with tools and camping gear. For some time he had been spending two or three days each week exploring the mountains, looking for the lode he was sure was the fountainhead of the gold in the gulch.

"How long this time?" Cushman asked.

"Two, three days, unless I find something promising." Dunbar dismounted and walked over to the sluice. "Doing any good?"

"I suppose."

"You suppose!" Dunbar grinned. "How much have you got in an Arbuckle's can under your bunk? Five thousand?"

"Not that much." Cushman leaned on his shovel. There was a warmth in Dunbar that pleased him. He was glad when the man was around. For the first time in his life Cushman was admitting to himself that he liked a man at the time of knowing him and not after leaving him.

Suddenly Dunbar's face was sober. "I asked her to marry me."

"How'd you ever get the chance?"

"After you and Big John left last night, while she was padlocking the back door." Dunbar kept waiting for Cushman to make a comment. "Don't you want to know what she said?"

"Sure."

"She said no." Dunbar smiled ruefully. "That wasn't the first time I asked her."

101

Cushman shrugged. He watched the clear water washing the heavy gravel in the sluice.

"When are *you* going to ask her, Ed?"

"Me!"

"Who the hell else am I talking to?"

"I ain't the marrying kind, Jake."

"I knew a lot of men like that in the Army. Every one of them has got a family now."

Cushman shook his head. "She wouldn't want me."

"Uh-huh," Dunbar said, and his meaning was not clear. "You ever been married?"

"No."

"I didn't know. I know who you are now and what you are now and that's about all." Dunbar gave Cushman a long appraisal. "That's quite a bit, I guess." He turned toward the horses. "Sleep kind of light, with one ear cocked toward her cabin while I'm gone, huh?"

"I generally do." Cushman watched Dunbar ride up the gulch.

A loud curse came from down the creek. Cushman saw Russian Bob come through the doorway of his saloon, struggling with a man. The man tried to draw a pistol. Russian Bob took it away from him and threw him from the high porch into the creek, and then stood looking down at him for a few moments. Miners along the creek looked up with interest, until the man stumbled out of the water and sat down on the bank.

Ask her to marry him? Cushman had considered the idea warily, but how would Dunbar have known that? She would refuse, of course; everything in Cushman's life had been refusal of some kind, starting at Gravelly Crossing. You protected yourself by not making requests of life that would be refused, no matter how much you desired something.

Cushman went back to shoveling into the sluice, but now and then he found himself leaning on his shovel and looking toward the restaurant, thinking of Belle Drago. He did not go to the restaurant for supper. He cooked in his cabin and found the food greasy and unpalatable, although it was about as good as any he had ever cooked.

He sat in his draughty cabin watching the fireplace burn down to grayness. Some time in a man's life there must be a chance to change, to get out of the channel that carried him on and on toward nothing, but how was he to recognize the chance when it came, or to make it deliberately?

The noises of Victory came through the cabin walls. For a while after Cushman's first wild night here, it had been a quiet place where tired men turned in at dark, with perhaps only a late card game going on at Big John's place or in someone's cabin; but now there was an uproar in Russian Bob's half the night and petty thievery was common.

Cushman went to bed. Several times in the last month there had been disturbances near Belle Drago's cabin in the night, and he and Dunbar, and Kenton, who slept in the wagon near her quarters, had roused out quickly to make sure that no one was trying to force his way into her cabin.

That night the dream of the demon bird of Indian legend came again to Cushman. He was a boy again, struggling through the night with his little sister in his arms, when the great bird came whistling down and tried to take her from him. He awoke in a cold sweat and stared into the blackness of the room, lonely and tormented.

The camp was quiet. He heard the murmur of the creek and the gentle soughing of the wind in the trees.

He went back to sleep thinking of Rumsey Snelling and his filthy, bearded face and his whining voice. *We got to help each other, Eddie boy . . . Eddie boy . . .*

Then Rumsey called out to him in terror, "Ed! Ed!" Cushman was wide awake again. The dream had the sharp edge of reality. He heard other sounds, a scuffling somewhere outside and the low, grunting noise of a man's voice.

It was the sharpness of the first noise that still hung in his mind as he put on his boots and pants and went outside. The door made a rattling noise as it drifted back against the jamb. A light was burning in a tent across the creek. The rest of the camp was dark. From Stapp's livery there came the sound of a horse blowing hay dust from its nostrils.

Cushman was about to go inside when he heard the muffled cry from the trees behind the cabin. "Ed!" and then there was the sound of a blow and the noise of scraping branches. It was Belle Drago's voice.

Cushman ran with fear and anger driving him. In the darkness of the trees he heard a man crashing away.

The fellow had been out in the darkness longer than Cushman, and he knew where he was going. He crossed a little opening going toward the south fork of Campanero Creek and was lost in the timber on the other side when Cushman reached the clearing. Cushman heard a branch crack sharply and then there was silence.

He went back through the trees toward where he had heard Belle Drago call out. He found her entangled in the bushes, trying to haul herself up by hanging to the branches of a tree.

"It's me—Cushman." He pulled her free of the bushes and her clothing tore as he helped her from the tangle. "Are you all right?" he asked harshly, afraid.

"Yes." She sagged against Cushman suddenly and he felt the fear and trembling in her.

"Who was it?"

"I don't know, Ed."

"How'd you get out here?"

"I couldn't sleep. I was walking—"

"In the trees? My God!"

"No! I was in the street. The man came out of the darkness— I don't know where he was hiding."

"Kenton?" Cushman asked.

"Not Joe Kenton, no!" Belle Drago stood away from Cushman. "Thank you. I'm all right now." She started away. Cushman caught her as she stumbled. He picked her up in his arms and went toward the street. One sleeve of her blouse was ripped. Her arm was bare and warm against Cushman's neck.

He walked stiffly, hurrying.

"No," she said, "not my cabin. I want to go to the restaurant. It's almost time to start the fire, anyway."

"That damned restaurant," Cushman muttered, and then wondered why he had said it.

He put her down at the back of the restaurant. She opened the door so quickly he wondered where she kept the key. He knew when she lit a lamp inside. The key was on a thin chain around her neck. The front of her blouse was torn. There were bruises around her mouth and a growing lump on her forehead.

As the light came up Cushman saw how frightened and shaken she was. She kept tugging her blouse up and fingering her bruised mouth.

"Where's Kenton?" Cushman asked.

"I had to let him go this evening."

Cushman swung around and strode out to the wagon. In the bed of it he stumbled over someone lying on the floor. He lit a lamp. Kenton was sprawled out on his stomach where he had fallen just short of reaching his cot. Cushman rolled him over. Kenton had been in a fight, and it looked as if he had got the short end of it.

After several minutes Cushman knew that the man was dead drunk. He probably had not stirred after he climbed the short ladder and pitched forward on the floor.

When Cushman went back to the restaurant Belle Drago had draped an apron over her shoulders and pinned it in front to cover her torn blouse. She was building a fire in the stove. Most of her self-control was back.

"You've no idea who it was?" he asked.

"None."

"It wasn't Kenton."

"I knew that."

"Why'd you fire him?"

"I had to let him go. It wasn't fair to keep him here doing this kind of work." Belle Drago hesitated. "He asked me to marry him tonight."

The hope of marrying her was the only reason that had kept Kenton around, Cushman thought. She had used him and caused him to be jeered at, but at least she had made an honest break with him at last. Kenton had gone through his own hell; you couldn't blame him for getting drunk.

Belle Drago dumped coffee into two huge pots already filled with water. She put more wood into the stove and then she turned to face Cushman. "I know what you're thinking, that I led Kenton on and used him. That was what was bothering me tonight, why I was walking when I should have been asleep."

Cushman glanced at the window. It would be light in another half-hour. He guessed he'd better stay that long.

"I know I'm out of place here," the woman said. "It would be all right if I were working myself to death for some man. That would be perfectly normal and proper."

"Why are you doing it?"

"To be independent."

Cushman could appreciate that, but there were bad flaws in her position.

Once more the woman seemed to read his mind. "If it weren't for men like you and Dunbar and Big John, I couldn't stay here. You've all protected me, and Kenton too. I suppose you're laughing to yourself because I stand behind your protection and then claim I'm free and independent."

"You're saying it, not me."

Belle Drago stared at Cushman in exasperation. "Do you ever say anything, Ed Cushman?"

"That key. You wear it around your neck." It was generally something dear or sacred that people wore on chains around their neck.

"It represents independence, not this miserable place where I work myself so tired I can't sleep sometimes. It means not having to ask anyone for anything, except when it can't be helped."

"I see." Cushman walked over to the window, as if to hurry the dawn. "You'd never give it up, would you?"

Belle Drago did not answer. When he turned to look at her she was studying him quietly. "Yes," she said, "I'd like to give it up but I don't think I ever can."

"You could marry Big John."

"Yes."

"Or Jake Dunbar."

"Yes."

Cushman saw the trees taking shape slowly outside. "Or me," he said.

Again the woman waited, forcing him to turn and look at her before she answered. "No, I couldn't marry you."

It was like coming back to the useless wagon at Gravelly Crossing. It was like seeing Beth Clendenin waving to him without meaning as she went away on the California trail. It was all the refusals and all the loneliness of Cushman's life rushing before him and telling him that this was the way it would always be and that he was a fool to hope for anything different.

His face was grave and without any expression of hurt as he nodded carefully. "I can understand that."

He thought Belle Drago was going to cry. She was pitying him and that was the last thing that he needed from anyone.

"You *don't* understand, Ed, and I can't tell you."

"Sure." It was light enough outside now to leave her alone. Cushman went over to the door.

"You didn't eat supper here last night, Ed."

"No."

"There were almost a hundred men, but I noticed that you—"

"I was busy, I guess." There was no use for her to tell him that she had missed his presence in the line of a hundred miners filing past the serving window. It would make no difference in the way Cushman felt because of her refusal.

He went on out. He stood a moment in the cold light, wondering why he had broken his protective shell long enough to be hurt.

CHAPTER TWELVE

THE MINERS' MEETING held in the back room of Big John Freemantle's saloon on the evening of the day Jake Dunbar returned from a four-day trip to the mountains was not to discuss the attempted rape of Belle Drago, for knowledge of that incident, as far as Cushman knew, was still confined to Belle, himself and the assailant.

With scarcely a decision involved, Cushman knew that he would kill the man if he ever found out who it was.

Only fifteen men were present, the veterans of the camp who had lived out the winter in the snows, and who also owned most of the gold taken from Victory. By common assent Dunbar was the chairman, and it was he who had insisted that Cushman attend.

There had been a great deal more thievery, robbery and attempted robbery than Cushman had known about, he discovered as he listened to conversations before the meeting was called to order. There was a general tone of suspicion against a group of ten or twelve men who had cabins and huts and tents on the west fork of Campanero Creek.

Dunbar called the meeting to order by banging the poker against the side of Big John's stove. "The way I get it, we ain't here to consider all the hell-raising in one lump. The thing that seems to be worrying most of us is the gold we've piled up since last summer.

"Most of us feel, the way things are going, it's getting more dangerous every day to keep it here. The question is, shall a bunch of us take it out to Denver, or shall every man be responsible for his own cache, or do we take a chance and have one or two men run it to Denver for us? Who's got some idea on the subject?"

It seemed dead simple to Cushman: let every man take care of his own gold.

Frank Eddy said, "I don't favor a whole bunch of us making the trip. This camp ain't going to last much longer, so I'd like to stay here and get in every day I can while there's still something to run through my sluice."

Handy Grimes was of the same opinion. "When I leave I aim to leave for good, but while I'm here I want to get everything I can off my ground."

"If the whole bunch of us takes off to carry the gold into Denver, somebody is going to be working our ground while we're gone," Mark Allen said.

"But you do want to get your gold where it'll be safe?"

"Damn right," Allen said. "I've had men prowling around my shack several times at night, and it's got so I spill half of every shovelful I start to put in my sluice, just from trying to watch my cabin."

Cushman listened in silence as they talked over the propositions.

Pete Eliot said, "I move we send two men out with the gold. We can pay 'em for the time they lose. Them that don't want to take the chance can take care of their own gold."

"I'm for that idea," Allen said. "I move Andy Volgamore be one of the men."

"Second the motion!"

Volgamore was a tall, hard-jawed ex-cavalry officer. It was he who had first discovered gold on Campanero Creek. "I dunno," he said. "I might decide to go clear to my old man's farm in Minnesota and bury the stuff."

"You'll have company about that time," Handy Grimes said, and there was a laugh.

"Let's have one motion at a time. First, we got to get a second to having two men take care of the gold." Dunbar looked around the room.

It took a pile of jawing to get a few simple matters settled, Cushman thought. With the rest, he raised his hand in an "aye" vote on both propositions.

Big John came into the room, pausing at the door to look back into the saloon. Dunbar explained briefly what had happened so far.

"I've a little dust of my own to send out," the saloon-man said. He looked at Cushman. "I'll move to make Ed Cushman the second man."

"I'll back that!" Eliot said.

Cushman was surprised that Big John had named him, but it was not the first time men had tried to thrust their responsibility on him, and generally he had refused. Now he saw Dunbar looking at him in appeal, urging him to take on the task, and Big John seemed to be challenging him to accept.

They were the only ones in the room who appeared to doubt that Cushman would agree; the others acted as if the matter were already settled.

"You'll do it, Ed?" Dunbar asked.

Cushman surprised himself by saying, "I guess so."

They voted him into the job while he was still wondering what it was he thought he owed them.

"What about splitting the two men up?" Eddy suggested. "Each one taking half, say?"

"Hell no!" someone said. "That's taking too big a chance that we'll lose half the gold and I don't want it to be the half that my sacks are in."

The statement evoked a hot discussion about means of decoying robbers away from the gold. There were all kinds of suggestions but nothing was settled. Eddy said, "I don't want to sit here all night and leave my cabin unguarded. Let's appoint a committee to work out the details and then we can agree on them in the next few days. We don't want to be making any fast moves right after this meeting anyway."

They agreed on a committee of five, Dunbar and four others. The meeting was starting to break up when Dunbar said, "Just one more thing. Miss Drago might want to be in on this. Is it all right to ask her? She's been sending some gold out with the Kenton brothers, but she told me the other day that they're getting leary of carrying it."

"Sure," Eliot said, "if she's willing to pay her share of the expense of Volgamore and Cushman."

"She pays her way," Big John said.

It was agreed that Dunbar could include Belle Drago in the project. The meeting broke up.

Dunbar caught up with Cushman in the dark outside the back door of the saloon. Lew Thompson, who had been on guard outside against eavesdroppers, said that no one had tried to get close to the back end of the building. He went to the edge of the creek with Dunbar and Cushman and then turned off toward his cabin.

"I got something to talk to you about, Ed." Dunbar's voice was both cautious and enthusiastic.

They were approaching Cushman's cabin when someone ran from it and went pounding into the trees. Cushman grabbed for his pistol before he remembered that he had left it in his bunk. Dunbar was armed and he drew his pistol. Cushman saw it poised in the starlight, but the intruder had run around the west side of the cabin and into the timber so quickly that firing would have been only a gesture.

Cushman's bunk was torn up, the cupboard door was swinging open, the ashes had been raked from the fireplace and the stones beneath turned up, and someone had probed with a pick in the floor around the bunk. Cushman threw the blankets back in place and found his pistol.

He wondered thinly why a miserable thief assumed that a man slept with his gold; Cushman's gold was buried just outside the sill log at the door.

"He get anything?" Dunbar asked.

Cushman shook his head.

Dunbar sat down on the bunk. "You act like you wouldn't give a damn if he had. Gold mean that little to you?"

"Not exactly. I can always use it."

"What if he'd got it?"

Cushman shrugged. "Then it would be gone." He found a bottle of whisky on a shelf above the fireplace. He picked up two tin cups the prowler had knocked into the woodbox.

Dunbar swirled the whisky in his cup with a circular motion of his hand. "How much dust have you got?"

"Maybe two, three thousand."

"Good." Dunbar went outside with the cup in his hand. Cushman heard him walk all the way around the cabin slowly. When he came back in Dunbar put one foot on a stool and took his drink. "I think I've found the lode where the gold in this gulch came from."

So that was it? Cushman felt a quick rise of pleasure.

If anyone deserved to realize a dream, Dunbar was the man.

"I think I'm on to a big thing," Dunbar continued. He took a piece of rusty rock from his pocket and gave it to Cushman. "Pound that up in a mortar and pan it and you'll see a string of gold as long as your finger. The outcrop stands three feet wide on the face of the mountain —not all of it as rich as that piece, but when you get deeper it ought to open up into the biggest thing that ever hit this country."

Cushman looked at the rock curiously. Lode mining was an expensive and long-term operation; it was not like a quick clean up of placer gold with a minimum of tools.

"I'll figure on a smelter in time," Dunbar said. "There'll be a railroad up this valley and a spur will run right over to the smelter and a town will spring up—"

"Not so fast, Jake."

"Not all at once, of course." Dunbar paced between the door and the fireplace. "I don't know anything about lode mining. Who does? You've got to start, just like every man running a sluice here had to find out the best way he could what he was trying to do." He grinned. "I've already ordered some tools, drills and black powder and a few things to get started with."

"I hope you hit it." Cushman put the piece of rock on the table.

"How'd you like to come in on it with me, Ed?"

"Why me?"

Dunbar was surprised. "You're my friend. What other reason do you need?"

Something turned in Cushman. He could not remember that anyone had ever said outright to him that he was a friend. It was a new, pleasant experience—and the feeling was not to be trusted too readily. "Who else is in on it with you?"

"Nobody," Dunbar said.

"I don't have a lot of money."

"You told me that. I guessed about what you had anyway. I've got maybe twelve thousand. By the way, when you and Volgamore take the gold into Denver, I want you to bank mine and bring back three thousand in cash— notes if you can get 'em. That will get us started on the mine."

"All right."

Dunbar leaned forward. "Are you going in with me?"

"I was thinking of leaving."

Dunbar nodded. "I guessed that."

"You did, huh?" Cushman waited for Dunbar to say more. He waited for the man to ask him what he was running away from, as others had, including Billy Bodega. And there had been a woman in New Mexico who had accused Cushman of being sorry for himself. It was the cheap and easy thing to say, and it had worried Cushman, but after thinking it over for a long time he knew he wasn't sorry for himself.

It was, rather, that he didn't know how to change his loneliness, how to lose his suspicions that a rebuff waited him for every favor asked of life. Maybe here was the chance to make the first real move.

Cushman didn't weigh the chances of success in the proposition Dunbar offered; he knew very little about lode mining. He wasn't even interested in making a fortune. But Dunbar wanted him in on the deal; Dunbar was showing him proof of friendship.

"All right," Cushman said. "I'll go in with you."

"Good." Once more Dunbar showed shrewd insight into Cushman's nature. "There'll be just the two of us. We'll split the profits on the basis of what each invests. Fair enough?"

Cushman nodded. "I wouldn't want it any other way." He felt the stirring of warmth and a new hope. Maybe settling down for a while was what he needed, fighting toward a dream, although at the moment he was not vitally interested in the dream itself. He suspicioned that Dunbar knew him very well, that Dunbar was working shrewdly to change him; but there was no doubting the man's friendship and good intentions.

And suddenly Cushman realized, too, that he had no wish to run away from Belle Drago, even if she *had* turned him down. He was getting his meals at her restaurant again, passing in line with a hundred other miners, but he knew that she was aware of him; and he was very much aware of the fact that the man she now had to help her in place of Joe Kenton was one whom Big John had found for her.

"We've settled that, then," Dunbar said. "In the next few days we'll let everybody know what the committee works out on the business we talked about tonight."

The next day the whole camp knew that a man named James Webster, a relative newcomer but a man who had a fair claim, had been robbed in the night. Several men had entered his tent when he was asleep, wrapped him in blankets and held him while they searched for his gold. They found it, five hundred dollars in dust, Webster had said.

Some of the veteran miners were doubtful about a man named Garvey, who had once worked for day's-pay on Webster's claim; but there was no real evidence against Garvey, he was a likable man, and he swore that he had been sound asleep when the robbery occurred. The camp growled and buzzed with anger but no one was brought to justice.

Dunbar's committee worked out their plan and kept the details secret. Those of the veterans who wished to send their gold to Denver were to bring it unobtrusively to Dunbar's cabin, where two men would always be on guard. They would get a receipt for it and after that they would have to trust the men they had appointed.

Since he was one of the two men in whom the veterans had placed final trust in the matter, Cushman felt that he could do no less than the others. He took his gold to Dunbar's cabin one night, and the next morning he took his turn with Andy Volgamore standing guard over the sacks for six hours.

"Tiresome as picket duty," Volgamore grumbled. He dozed part of the time but he was trigger-sharp and awake the instant anyone came near the cabin.

CHAPTER THIRTEEN

ONE EVENING while Cushman and Dunbar were sitting on Pete Eliot's sluice box eating their supper, Dunbar said, "Meet me at nine tomorrow at the waterfall, straight up the main creek."

Cushman nodded. He and Volgamore were going out with the gold.

Dunbar came alone to the appointed place with two horses from Stapp's livery. One of them was carrying camping gear and tools. Dunbar led the horse into the trees where Cushman was waiting. He took the tools off the pack but left the camping gear.

"Where's Volgamore?"

Dunbar shook his head. "That's something else. Cut over clear beyond the west fork, Ed, and go out by way of Trout Creek Pass. Take it through, of course, but remember if you get in a bad fix—it's only gold."

"What does that mean?"

"Damn it!" Dunbar was nervous and unhappy. "No one expects you to get killed over it!"

"Neither do I." Cushman gave the horses critical appraisal.

"They're the best we could do without rousing too much suspicion," Dunbar said. "As it was, Bert Garvey looked me over pretty close when I left camp. Maybe it was just my nerves. Unless I'm followed, I'll stall around up here all morning. Four hours' start should be enough, shouldn't it?"

"Sure." Cushman hesitated. "Is Belle sending in anything?"

"Yes."

Cushman rode away, holding to the scattered parks along the base of the mountains until he was well around the west fork of Campanero. He picked his way through the timber then and went on down into the valley. Freighters going up-river to Cache Creek or Georgia Bar or California Gulch, where men had washed out millions, were raising dust above the sage and rabbit brush.

The blue timber that hid the gulch where Victory lay fell farther upslope on the snow-patched mountains, and the brown rocks of Trout Creek Pass came closer. There was no dust on Cushman's trail.

It was a good day.

Cushman had ridden free in wide valleys like this before, going nowhere. Today there was something solid and satisfying in the trip; he knew where he was going, and why, and he knew where he was returning to.

He did not crowd the horses. They were not the kind that could make a hard run over the long distance ahead.

After a time he decided that the horses were sorrier specimens than he had thought at first. The bay pack horse had been badly shod and now it was developing a slight limp in the right foreleg. The animal he was riding was hard-gaited. It showed a tendency to want to stop and forage.

In a grove of cottonwoods beside a cold stream he rode into a camp of freighters who were repairing a wheel tire that had worn thin and broken. He passed the time of day with them while he let his horses water. The efforts of the freighters around a rude forge they had set up against a cottonwood tree bothered him. The tire they were working on was what Sam Hildreth used to call "dish-ironed," which meant there was a soft spot in it that wore out sooner than the rest of the iron.

Cushman watched with the nervous unease of a craftsman who sees work being badly done. The part of the splice already made in the tire had the flaky aspect of having been burned, and now they were trying to set in the other end of the section without enough heat.

Cushman walked to the edge of the grove and looked up-river. He went back to the forge. "I used to do some blacksmithing, boys. Maybe I could give you a hand."

A hulking teamster who was scowling at the efforts of his companions as he pumped a bellows suspended from the tree quit working the pole lever and sized up Cushman, and then he grabbed the hammer from the hand of the man who had been using it. "I'm glad to see someone who knows iron from horse manure." The freighter whipped sweat out of his beard and gave the hammer to Cushman. "Fire away, mister!"

The bellows leaked and the iron they were using as an anvil was badly chipped, like the hammer, but Cushman forgot those handicaps when he saw the fine, even glow of good Pittsburgh forge coal. He called for a longer section of iron to set into the tire. With the help of the freighters he reheated the burned splice and cut back from it. He made the splice on that end over again, then wrapped a wet gunny sack around it and reheated the other end of the inset.

The big freighter said, "You've had forge soot in your snoot before, mister."

Cushman scrubbed his work in the dirt so he could see what kind of joining he had made. It was good. It would have been neater with better tools, but it was good.

The freighters wanted him to stay for dinner. They had shot two antelope on their way from Denver and now they offered to barbecue them both and, with a keg of whisky, make a day of it. Cushman grinned and said he had to meet a man down the river in an hour.

He rode back on his trail and had another look at the hills to the northwest. They were clear of dust. He felt fine as he resumed his trip.

The first pass he had to cross was merely a low break in the hills. Horses in average condition could take it easily, but the horses he had were not even average, and there were long miles beyond the first pass. Why not go on down to the ranch and get his own horses and leave the worn-down livery nags? He had lost an hour with the freighters and he would lose more time switching horses, but he would make it up later.

The decision pleased him. There was satisfaction, too, in the ease with which he had repaired the tire. It was, he repeated to himself, a good day.

He lost a little more time than he had figured on at the ranch, because his horses were hiding out in dense willows on a creek, but at last he and the rancher caught them. Cushman took his own saddle and left the warped livery rig to be picked up on his return. Fording the Arkansas at a wide gravel bar, he went up the east bank toward the pass.

It occurred to him that he could get a present for Belle in Denver, something she couldn't refuse in spite of her stiff pride. He was thinking of that when he started up the small green-edged stream on Trout Creek Pass.

His horses had come through the late spring in good shape. They were not fat and they were full of energy. They would get him to Denver half a day earlier than the ones he had left behind. They went up the winding stream among the rocks with a will, but after he had gone half a mile, the compression of limited distance ahead and behind began to worry him.

He turned up a sandy gulch and went to the top of a hill on the north side of the pass. From there he could look across the valley and clear on to the fold of the gulch he had left this morning.

With a coldly thoughtful expression he saw the dust of several riders just entering the grove where the freighters were. He waited and watched the riders break out soon afterward on the other side. He considered the idea of quick flight. Unless they had far better horses than he thought they had, he could increase the miles between them from here to Garo, where he could undoubtedly get fresh horses. By stripping everything from the pack horse but the gold, he could make a straight-out race of it without stopping anywhere to change horses, but there was the chance that the pursuers might change horses themselves.

With growing anger, Cushman watched the dust cloud. The horsemen might not be after him at all. He remembered a wagon train that had almost killed their oxen coming into Ruby Valley after mistaking dust devils for Indian smoke signals. Cushman was not going to run from nothing. In fact, he was not going to run at all.

He eased the cinch on his saddle. He dumped the camping gear from the pack horse and led the animal close to a high, flat rock and dragged the panniers of gold off it.

He saw the distant riders stop where his trail to the ranch met the fork of the pass road. They milled around for several minutes. Two riders went on toward the ranch. The rest came straight toward the pass.

Cushman left the camping gear. He dragged the gold back on the pack horse. For half a mile he made a hard run with the horses until he found the place he wanted, a narrow, sandy gulch with steep rocky sides. He dismounted to cross it. On the far side he turned to his left and went on up into the piñons and tied the horses.

With his rifle he settled down about sixty yards away from where he had crossed the gulch. He chose a sitting position between two rocks that were spaced with a narrow gap commanding the gulch. He had never run because of physical fear. When men thought they had you on the go they were like coyotes after a crippled deer.

Men had trusted him with their gold. He had accepted the responsibility and he would carry it. There was a bigger risk in running than in making his stand now.

When he heard them coming they were risking the legs of their horses in the rocks as if they thought they were closing in. He knew they had seen the abandoned camping gear and thought he was running for it. He heard a man say, "He'll beat us to the park, all right, but we'll change horses and run him down before he hits the Platte."

They were crowding each other as they came into the narrow gulch. Augie Reynolds was in the lead, a tall, handsome man who owned a paying claim on one of the branches of Campanero Creek. He raised his hand in a cavalry signal and yelled, "Don't rush it here, boys!" He looked up the gulch for a better crossing and for a time he was staring at the rocks where Cushman lay concealed. Then he swung down and began to lead his horse where Cushman's tracks showed.

Close behind him was Ennis Judson, and this could have been expected, Cushman thought, for Judson hung around the saloons in Victory, watching the gambling tables and the size of the pokes of the miners who played there. There were three others whom Cushman had seen but did not know. One of them, the last one, hesitated before going down into the gulch, seeking out an easier route than the others had followed. Cushman waited a split second longer. He wanted them all dismounted if possible.

Then Reynolds saw the tracks turning northward. He said, "Hey! There's something—"

Cushman shot him through the chest. He tried then for the man still mounted, still hesitating on the right side of the gulch, and missed the snap shot. The rider wheeled his horse and in one lunge was out of sight. Cushman fired into the mass of animals in the gulch. A horse snorted and reared and fell. Cushman saw the man who had been trying to mount it go spinning backward against a rock.

Someone fired twice at Cushman but the sounds only added to the confusion in the gulch. A riderless horse lunged up the bank and trampled Reynolds as it bolted away. Judson tried to scramble up the right bank on foot, his pistol in his hand as he ran. Cushman shot again and saw him tumble back into the gulch.

It was over then and Cushman still had ammunition left. One man had led his horse between the narrow squeeze of rocks down gulch and was riding away. Cushman stood up and walked slowly toward the scene. Judson had a broken leg. He was lying on his back, blinking at the sun. With shock fogging his expression, he rolled his head and said, "Hello, Cushman," as if they were old friends.

Augie Reynolds was dead. Cushman knew the horse that had trampled him must have tried to miss him as it surged away but it had crushed his face.

The man who had been hurled against a rock as he tried to mount his plunging horse now sat up and groaned, holding his back with both hands. He was gray in the face, and he held his head down toward one shoulder as he rocked back and forth. Cushman took away his weapons and kicked him to his feet. "Who are the two that went toward the ranch?"

"I don't know what you mean."

Cushman cocked his rifle and held it stomach-high on the fellow.

"Bert Garvey and Len Ebersole," the man said.

"And the two that got away right here?"

"Stub Manders and Mossy Brown." The man looked down at Judson. "You killed Augie, and look what you did to Jud. You had no call to run hog-wild, Cushman. I'm beginning to think you don't have the gold after all. I think, by God, we've been tricked!"

They were a sorry pair, the one gray and sick, and Judson lying in the hot sand with his leg twisted out from his body. These two and Reynolds were done. The two survivors most likely had their purpose jarred completely awry. To make sure, Cushman would stop again farther up the pass.

"Hey! You can't leave me here with Judson hurt like that!"

"Tell that to your friends."

When Cushman reached the horses he saw dust coming from the direction of the ranch—Garvey and Ebersole. He judged Garvey as the kind of man who lacked the guts to resume the chase once he found out what had happened to his friends. The other two, Brown and Manders, were of unknown mettle.

Cushman went on up the pass and set another trap. Anger carried him for a time and then a reaction set in. There was nothing pleasant about shooting men. If you had to you did so, but it was a brutal business.

He waited until he was sure that his savage ambush there in the narrow gulch had broken up the pursuit.

The remark the man had made about his not having the gold stuck in his mind. He had stopped with the freighters; the pursuers surely had found that out, and it must have made them wonder about his seeming lack of urgency. He went back to the horses. While he had been waiting he had hoisted the small leather panniers off the pack horse with a rope run over a tree limb.

Now he backed the horse under the weight again and

let the panniers down. It was a lot of money that he was responsible for. What had made that fellow with the injured back doubt that he had the gold?

The poor quality of the horses originally provided for the trip . . . was that actually part of the ruse? Dunbar's remark about not fighting too hard to protect the gold had been odd.

Cushman unstrapped the top of one of the panniers and removed several of the sacks. He knew at once that their weight was not right for that much bulk of gold. Fastened to the tie around the neck of each sack was a tag. Cushman opened the pouch with Handy Grimes's name on it. He took a pinch from the inside.

Sand.

He dumped some of the contents into the palm of his hand. Sand. He spilled the pouch into the bunch grass at his feet.

One by one he tried half a dozen sacks. They were all filled with sand. He saw the faces of the men whose names were on them. A coldness settled in him and he knew that those men had used him as a decoy without telling him so. It had been shame, not nervousness, that had made Dunbar so edgy.

Cushman unloaded the panniers, tossing the sacks aside after he glanced at the names. There were several pouches with Dunbar's name on the tags and several others with Belle Drago's name. Cushman tossed both sets back into the panniers and left all the others on the ground.

All of them had let him risk his life for nothing. They had sent him out to kill men over sand. Dunbar and Belle were the ones that had hurt him most.

Dunbar should have told him, and then Cushman would have made a run for it, instead of stopping deliberately to kill men.

Cushman leaned against the pack horse and tried to fight down his blackness of spirit with reason. Dunbar had known that he was to be only the decoy and had tried to hint that it was so; maybe there were reasons why he could not tell Cushman the truth.

It didn't work out: there were no reasons that Cushman could understand why, at the last moment, he could not have been told the truth—except that the miners had not trusted him. Even Dunbar had not trusted him. The few steps Cushman had taken toward faith in fellow human beings crumbled away. He was back where he had started, back to nothing; but now he knew the difference between nothing and what he had started to achieve.

He started back to Victory. For the second time he surprised the men who had pursued him. He came out of the rocks at the head of the narrow gulch where he had ambushed them and stopped with his rifle across his saddle, looking down on the scene for a few moments before they knew he was close.

Then they saw him. They stared up at him with sullen anger. Garvey and Ebersole were there and the two men who had got away during the shooting. They were trying to set Judson's leg. None of them made any move toward their weapons.

When the group fell silent Judson rolled his head and saw the reason. He cursed Cushman bitterly.

Cushman rode away into the piñons and stopped again, screened by the trees, waiting to see if anyone was disposed to follow him. None of them moved; they had had enough of him. He heard Judson accuse Garvey. "You gave us a bum steer, Garvey. You didn't know what you were talking about."

Cushman went on toward Victory. He was not followed.

At the grove of cottonwoods where he had stopped to help the freighters he heard shouts and laughter. Apparently they had gone ahead with their barbecue. Cushman wondered at the childish pleasure he had taken in showing off his skill before them.

He rode wide around the grove and went on up the lonely valley.

CHAPTER FOURTEEN

It was dark when Cushman rode into Victory. Russian Bob's place was roaring and there seemed to be a larger crowd than usual in Big John's saloon. He went on to the restaurant. Through the window he saw Belle Drago putting pans of bread in the warming oven. Her new helper was scrubbing the floor.

Cushman took the panniers from the pack horse and walked in without knocking. Belle swung around to stare at him. The swamper leaned on his mop, sensing Cushman's mood instantly and afraid of it.

Cushman dumped the panniers on a work table. "I brought your gold back, Belle. Dunbar's too." He turned and started out.

"Ed!" Belle came swiftly across the room. She gave the sacks on the table a quick look. "Wait a minute, Ed."

Cushman looked at her quietly. It was understandable that she didn't care to marry him, but he had done his best to earn her trust.

"Go find Jake Dunbar and bring him here. Quick!" Belle said to her helper. The youth leaned his mop against the wall and hurried away, stepping carefully around Cushman.

The woman met Cushman's dark look without flinching. There was no shame in her, no fear. He saw how tired she was from the day's work. Her appraisal of him was gentle, almost sad.

"It was a bad trip?" she asked.

"I killed a man—over sand."

"Who?"

"Augie Reynolds," Cushman said. He knew now why he had brought back only the sacks marked with the names of Belle Drago and Dunbar. They were the two people in Victory who meant something to him.

"The miners hanged one of Reynolds's friends here today, and ran several more of them out of camp," Belle said. "They found out that—" She saw that Cushman wasn't interested. "I didn't know that you were the one carrying the sacks of sand until Dunbar told me, long after you left."

Cushman said nothing.

"Why aren't you mad at the whole camp, Ed?"

"The whole camp doesn't count." Cushman saw fine lines of strain around Belle's mouth and eyes.

She said, "Sit down. I'll get some coffee. Jake will be here in a minute."

"What can he say?"

"Sit down and find out."

Dunbar came in a few minutes later. He looked from Belle to Cushman and needed no explanation. "I see you changed horses, Ed. I had some of the boys take 'em over to the livery for you. All right?" He picked up one of the sacks on the table and tossed it down again. "I couldn't tell you. It was part of the plan."

"Sure," Cushman said. He thought of the agony he had caused in that narrow gulch. That the pursuers deserved it was of no moment. Right now he felt more kinship for the men he had fought than for the miners who had tricked him.

"Why'd you come here to torment Belle?" Dunbar asked. "She didn't know what was going on until I told her, after you left." Once more he picked up a sack and let it drop on the table. For the first time since Cushman had known him, Dunbar was having trouble holding on to his temper.

Belle touched his arm. "Tell him everything, Jake."

"By God, I will. We made up two sets of pouches, one bunch with sand and the other the real stuff. The committee was afraid of itself. They put the last of it on me, even to picking the time to make the run.

"One of the sets of sacks was Heads, the other Tails. Over in Big John's back room, Frank Eddy and some of the boys flipped a coin. It came up Tails. That meant the runner going out by Trout Creek Pass was to carry the Tails panniers—the sand. That was you because we'd already flipped to see whether you or Volgamore went that way."

Dunbar spoke quietly, but anger was growing in his voice as he went on. "Volgamore was to go up-river and over Weston Pass. The thing of it was, when they flipped that silver dollar in Big John's place, nobody but me knew which set of sacks had the sand and which had the gold. That way none of the committee could be accused of tipping off the deal."

Dunbar gave Cushman a bitter look. "Nobody but me, that is. There was seventeen men in the thing, including Big John and Belle. There was right close to eighty thousand dollars in dust involved. I was the son of a bitch who knew which one of you was carrying it.

"I sweated blood until I came back to town and found out that Garvey had gone trotting over to the west fork and that Augie Reynolds and his bunch had taken out after you." Dunbar picked up Cushman's cup of coffee and drained it. "I did my best to tell you what you were carrying, although I wasn't even supposed to do that."

Deep inside Cushman felt shame. It was Dunbar they might have pulled to pieces if something had gone wrong. The committee of five had given him supreme trust, but if anything had slipped he would have been a scapegoat in an instant. Cushman knew now what a social conscience was.

"If they had taken after Volgamore, we had four horses left," Dunbar said, "but they were worse than the ones I gave you, and no match at all for the horses Reynolds's outfit had. We might not have been much help."

Cushman did not wish to face Belle's quiet look; it was enough to meet Dunbar's expression directly. Dunbar lifted one of the sacks and let it drop and kept staring at Cushman.

"I made a fool of myself," Cushman said.

"Yes, you did," Dunbar said flatly. "Trust is a two-way deal. You—"

"Never mind, Jake," Belle said.

"By God, I got as much patience as the next man," Dunbar said, "but when somebody—"

"Never mind, Jake," Belle said again gently, and Dunbar was silent, looking at Cushman with exasperation.

For the fourth time, Dunbar picked up one of the sacks and tossed it down hard in front of Cushman. It came through to Cushman then, something that he had missed when his anger crippled his normal perceptions when he was handling the sacks with Dunbar's name and Belle's name on the tags.

He hefted the sack in front of him. He looked quickly from Dunbar to the woman.

"Yes!" Dunbar said. "Yes, damn it!"

Cushman untied the sack. It bore Belle's name, and it held gold. He did not need to look at the others or even lift them.

"We didn't doubt that you'd go clear through to Denver," Belle said. "We knew how you'd feel. All Jake asked me was whether I wanted you to carry my gold. That's all he told me about the plan until afterward."

They sat looking at Cushman.

"I'm sorry," Cushman said. His face was solemn but he was so twisted up inside that he could say no more.

Belle rose suddenly. "I've got to watch my bread. I think my last batch of yeast was too strong."

"I'll check up to see they're giving your horses the

best," Dunbar said, "and I'll arrange for somebody to go down to that ranch and bring back the livery nags tomorrow."

Out in the darkness of the street Dunbar said, "What about Reynolds?"

Cushman told him the bare details.

"We hung a man here today over the Webster robbery," Dunbar said. "Caught him with the goods. We run some of the others out of town. It'll be a better camp now, Ed."

Cushman said, "Suppose they'd caught up with Volgamore and got the gold, then what would the miners think about you and Belle sending your dust with me?"

Dunbar had regained his good humor. "It would have looked bad, for a fact, wouldn't it?" He laughed. "Anyway, I would have made a beautiful speech just before they hanged me."

Cushman thought that some day he might be able to tell Dunbar about Gravelly Crossing.

CHAPTER FIFTEEN

JAKE DUNBAR lived in a fret and a fury until one day the Kenton brothers freighted in the tools he had ordered —two bellows, a duckfoot for a forge, drill steel, striking hammers, kegs of black powder and other items. Joe Kenton was working with his brothers now, but he never helped them unload when they delivered supplies to Belle Drago.

"First off, we'll need a blacksmith," Dunbar said.

"I can get by as a blacksmith," Cushman said.

"Fine!" Dunbar seemed to give the problem no more thought. "The first thing to do then is to get our tools up there and set up some kind of camp close to the mine. I hate to waste time building a trail but we'll have to have one. How many men shall we hire?"

"Let's take a look first."

They went up the mountain with two pack horses.

When they came to the stunted trees at timberline, Cushman looked at the gray slopes and wondered if there were tools enough in the world to make an impression on the mountain.

"How far up there?" he asked.

"About a mile," Dunbar said cheerfully. "You never mentioned knowing anything about blacksmithing."

"I learned a little about it from a man who took me in out in the Nevada country after my family died on the way to California." It was hard to say. Cushman waited for a quick reaction from Dunbar.

"What you learned is going to come in mighty handy." Dunbar looked up the mountain, squinting.

Cushman didn't know whether it was deliberate pretense on Dunbar's part or whether the man had accepted only that part of a hard statement which was of practical interest now. If he had probed, Cushman would have gone back into his shell. Dunbar had not probed. Still, Cushman felt some resentment about his lack of interest.

"I've ridden a horse part of the way up there," Dunbar said, "but it ain't worth it." He grinned. "Shall we start building trail right now, or do you want to have a look at—"

"Yeah. I'd like to see where we're going first."

It took them two hours to climb to the outcrop. Once they were there, Cushman was appalled by the roughness of that mile that lay between them and the timber. Victory itself lay hidden by the bend of a wooded ridge, but the lower end of the road into it was visible. They could see their horses quite plainly in an alpine meadow at timberline.

Dunbar was all over the face of the outcrop like an excited monkey, chipping rock, prying specimens loose with a short-handled pick. "Look at that!" he cried, waving at the outcrop. "Is there any reason it won't run as deep as the mountain?"

"Maybe deeper," Cushman said, and grinned. The mass of rusty-looking quartz was thrust out through iron-stained granite. Cushman had crushed and panned some of it and he knew it held free gold, a great deal of it. The showing was as wide, or even wider, than the three feet Dunbar had said. Cushman looked up the dizzying run of the mountain, past ledges and buttresses that ran to the sky. This seemed to be the only place where the quartz broke out.

Dunbar's word and his enthusiasm were enough. The

prospects of having a mine did not excite Cushman as much at the moment as the problem of building a trail up here around sheer drops and across rock fields that looked ready to slide away at the touch of a foot.

"There'll be a railroad up the valley some day," Dunbar said. "About where that crazy prospector is working a gravel bar, we'll take off with a spur, wind it around a couple of times in the timber, and—"

"You think *he's* crazy, do you?" Cushman looked down the mountain and shook his head.

Dunbar laughed and went on with his plans, and all the while Cushman kept working out in his mind the lines they must follow to build a trail up here. It would have to be wide enough for pack animals to carry timber. It was not going to be easy. The challenge began to grip him.

The next day they hired four men and started the trail where Cushman had planned while he was sitting at the Illinois, the name Dunbar had already given the mine. Neither of the partners nor the men they hired knew the first principle of drilling rock or blasting with black powder. Cushman discovered that the temper of the drills he sharpened was either too soft or too hard. They mushed to bluntness quickly in the former case and broke in the latter case. When he struck a temper that stood up well he was not sure how he'd done it.

A former quarryman from Vermont came up one day and watched the trail building, and then he stood in the doorway of the rough blacksmith shop at timberline, watching in silent pain until Cushman, sensing both the criticism and craftsmanship of the man, put one foot on the anvil block and said, "For God's sake, speak up!"

"You shape a good bit," the Vermonter said, "but the tempering is a crime. There's a way to drill rock and a way to temper steel."

"Do you want a job?"

The Vermonter considered. "I might."

Cushman hired him forthwith. His name was John Marvel. He had walked across the plains to Denver and from there to a dozen mining camps looking for work that suited him. Now he had it. He showed the trail builders how to drill, and after that it was a matter of acquiring skill by practice. Cushman took out the insurance of learning tempering from Marvel before he turned the shop over to him, and went up on the trail to work.

Marvel's coming was the key that unlocked progress. The trail went faster and faster, across the faces of cliffs, over slide rock that did not run as easily as Cushman had thought, and on up toward the golden promise of the outcrop.

It was not fast enough for Dunbar. He bought more tools and hired more men and gave them the advantages of instruction he had received himself from Marvel. To Dunbar, trail-building was almost a waste of time. He wanted to be down in the mountain, to see a railroad and a smelter. To speed up things he hired still more men and began to build trail from the Illinois down.

The gap between made all kinds of complications, but Dunbar had a chance to hammer and pound and knock specimens from the outcrop, and to look down to where the railroad spur would leave the main line, and to change the site of the smelter as it suited him day by day. Dunbar was completely happy.

Cushman was edging slowly toward satisfaction himself. He enjoyed swinging a double jack in the thin air, loading holes and hearing the muffled *poom* of black powder breaking rock where he wanted it broken. It was satisfying to look upon the steep fall of the mountain one day and then to see the next day a few more feet of trail reaching upward on the easy grade he'd planned.

He knew he lacked Dunbar's vision. Cushman was content to do a good job day by day, to plan his next step carefully. In giving orders to men he learned more about them and himself than he had ever learned before. He discovered that their respect and liking returned in approximately the same measure as given.

They laughed and joked with Dunbar and exchanged friendly insults, and asked him how soon he was going to start the smelter, and whether he was going to build his railroad spur first or wait for the main line from Denver. They were not as free and easy with Cushman, but still a startling fact was unfolding to him: they all liked him.

When the two sections of the trail began to near each other on the bleak granite, Dunbar set part of the crew to drilling the outcrop and soon they had more ore piled on the level place they had blasted out for mine buildings than the shelf would hold. Some of the ore tumbled down the mountain. Dunbar began to blast a bigger shelf.

Almost every miner in Victory had tested a piece of the ore. The camp agreed that Dunbar and Cushman had a big thing, but some thought the partners might be ahead of the times.

Standing in a cold wind one day at the mine, after the crew had gone down, Cushman asked Dunbar, "How's our money holding out?"

Dunbar cocked his head. "It's going faster than I thought it would." His volatility for once was capped and quiet as he stared from the mountain. The nearly finished trail, catching shadows now that the sun was on top of the mountains, the small piece of road at the lower end of Victory, and the shine of tiny green patches in the valley that marked two ranches were the only signs of men that the eye could see.

Distance put silence on everything.

Cushman knew that all their furious efforts had scarcely made a scratch on the mountain. From the valley when the light was right a man could barely see sections of the trail, if he knew exactly where to look, but the mine itself blended into the mountain and the greater mountains behind it so that it was nothing.

Watching Dunbar standing quietly in his ragged coat, with his shoulders hunched against the wind, Cushman wondered if his partner were thinking the same as he. Work here was like looking back during a desert crossing at a landmark which you knew was eight miles farther away each day but which seemed to grow no smaller.

Cushman didn't think their efforts were futile, by any means, but he knew how slowness galled Dunbar. Dunbar was as aware of daily problems as Cushman was, but his mind was geared to race on far ahead. If he had one smelter now, he would be planning ten more.

"You really think we're doing all right?" Cushman asked.

"We're doing fine. But I underestimated things. It'll take a lot more money and time than I expected."

"You've laid out four times as much as I have, haven't you?"

"I suppose. What's the difference? It's men that count, not money. You're the one I wanted for a partner. That was what was important. The money part is important only if we don't have enough of it." Dunbar turned his coat collar up. It was still dark blue on the underside.

He said, "I've been talking to Big John. Freight costs would ruin us if we tried to haul ore out of here." His voice gained strength and the assurance that had been missing for a time returned. "So we've got to build our smelter as soon as possible. It won't cost much to haul bullion."

"No, but what will it cost to build a smelter? Freight costs will hit us on every stick and timber and brick."

"I know," Dunbar said. "That's where Big John comes in. He knows people in England who'll be interested in a stock proposition. He knows two men who can raise a hundred thousand pounds selling stock. That's half a million dollars, Ed, but it's only money and that's what we need." He gave Cushman a questioning look. "We'll have to take Big John in as a full partner."

"Is that a squeeze?"

"No. It's just the fair thing. The three of us would have controlling interest."

Hostility between Cushman and Big John Freemantle was as strong as ever. It seemed to Cushman that since Belle's refusal to marry him, Big John had pressed his own cause harder. Cushman had been busy on the trail, staying most of his nights in the hut at the lower end. But Big John, with three bartenders now working for him, had been free to visit her in the restaurant almost every night.

It was a wrench to divorce these personal facts from Dunbar's plan. If it had been any man but Dunbar, Cushman might not have been able to make the break. "All right," he said, "take Big John in." He saw Dunbar's relief.

"He won't involve his friends in anything with too much gamble in it," Dunbar said. "Before he even makes a move on the stock deal, he wants the Illinois examined by two mining engineers, friends of his. They've been spending the summer around Idaho Springs." Dunbar shrugged carelessly. "I think it's a good idea. They can give us some hint of how really big the Illinois is. All right with you?"

"Sure."

Dunbar forgot the engineers at once. His eyes watered in the cold wind as he squinted down the mountain. "Do you suppose there's enough water on the east fork of

Campanero for the smelter? It's the best site if we can be sure about the water."

"How much water does a smelter need?"

"I don't know."

Cushman grinned. "Ask the engineers about it. Let's get off this mountain before dark." Dunbar would have put in twenty-four hours a day working and planning, if he could.

They scrambled across the unfinished part of the trail with the ease of familiarity. Walking ahead, Dunbar asked suddenly, "What was it with your folks, Indians?"

"Cholera."

"That's always bad. Diphtheria got most of my family, right at home during the war. My father and mother, my two younger brothers and one of my sisters—all within a week. It happened when I was in the Wilderness. I got wounded there and then damned near burned to death when the woods caught fire.

"It was eight months before I got out of the hospital and got home and found out what had happened. Pa and me had talked a lot about having our own butcher shop. For a while I thought I had to go ahead and get it, but when I got out here I knew I never would go back."

Dunbar spoke without bitterness or pain.

Maybe it was easier to forget such things if you hadn't been close to them when they happened. It was like a letter going back to some state from an emigrant trail, telling someone that a whole family had been wiped out. Elapsed time and distance softened the shock. Or did it? Maybe the uncertainty and helplessness were greater. They crossed the face of a cliff and Dunbar stopped to light his pipe where the trail curved against overhanging rocks. Cushman saw his expression and knew that coming home and being told that your family had died months before was no easier than being with them when they died. . . .

When they resumed their way Cushman's memory of Gravelly Crossing did not seem as black as before. He began to talk about it to Dunbar's back. No part of it came easily. He told it all. When he was recounting how he had returned to find the camp deserted and his father's wagon gone, his blood began to surge wildly and he cursed the Snellings, all of them, forgetting kindness even for the girl who had given him her pitifully hoarded food.

"It's been a long time in coming, hasn't it?" Dunbar said.

"What do you mean?"

"You've never told that story, have you?"

"How do you know?" Cushman had the feeling that somehow Dunbar had drawn the tale from him.

"If you had, you'd have run out long ago on cussing the Snellings. The woman did what she could. She couldn't have helped your sister, you admit. All they did was run out on you, not your whole family. From your description of them, maybe it was the best thing for you."

"The best thing! I ate mice and dead gulls, and I—"

"Who hasn't been hungry?" Dunbar asked. "I've been close to being a one-bite cannibal right here in the mountains. What do you want to do, kill all the Snellings because they were no good? If that's it, you should have done it long ago. I'd say you were lucky you got away from them. They might have raised you as a son."

Cushman grabbed Dunbar's shoulder and spun him around. He had an idea Dunbar was grinning. Dunbar was not smiling. Cushman was bewildered to see him coldly serious. "It's the Snellings that stick in your craw, Ed. You didn't get heated up or start to cuss until you mentioned the part where they left you. For every bastard that runs out on you in a fix, there's three good men who won't. You've never given anybody a chance to prove that. I'd say you've been a damned fool."

"You weren't there, Jake."

"How old were you?"

"Thirteen," Cushman said.

"You're not thirteen now." Dunbar turned and went on down the trail.

When they reached the hut they had built behind their blacksmith shop, Marvel was sitting on a stump in front of the canvas door, looking at the sunset. He knocked his pipe out carefully in his palm, looking for unburned tobacco fragments. "There's a venison stew ready." He looked at the sunset again. "Be out of forge coal in two weeks if we don't get some."

Cushman was restless. His telling about Gravelly Crossing had not relieved everything that he had thought it might. He said, "I'll go on into camp and leave word about the coal. The Kentons ought to be in tomorrow or the next day."

"Leave the word with Belle," Dunbar said. "She won't forget."

Cushman went down toward Victory. He had not expected sympathy from Dunbar, and he had not got it either—that was good. What had he expected? It came to him that no one could make him forget Gravelly Crossing and all the loneliness it had created in his life afterward. He would have to do the changing himself and arrive gradually at acceptance of what had happened. Maybe that was what Jake Dunbar had tried to show him.

The serving window and the front door of the restaurant were open to let out heat and cooking odors, but Cushman knew that service was finished for the day. He hesitated in the doorway. "Will you tell the Kentons we need three hundred pounds of forge coal, Belle?"

"Of course." The woman hung a pan on a nail behind the stove. "Have you had your supper, Ed?"

"Yes. I came down just to—"

"You haven't eaten, have you? You're not a very good liar, Ed Cushman. Come in and I'll find you something."

The helper finished scrubbing and went away to get the pails of water for Belle Drago's bath. A miner came to the door and asked if he could get a meal.

"The place is closed," Belle Drago said.

"What about him?" The miner was disposed to argue when he saw Cushman eating.

"The place is still closed."

Cushman turned his head to look. The miner recognized him and said, "Oh, him, huh? I see," and went away.

Cushman kept his eyes on his plate, strangely embarrassed because the man's words had suggested something which did not exist. "How's Joe Kenton?"

"All right, I guess."

"Did he get over you firing him?"

"That isn't why he hates me."

Cushman decided he had carried the subject far enough. After a time he asked, "You figure to be independent like this all your life?"

The woman didn't answer. She came across the room slowly and sat down opposite Cushman, and then she said, "Why did you ask that?"

"I wondered if you ever change your mind." It was as

close as Cushman could get to asking her to marry him again. In the quick set of her eyes he saw that she understood well enough.

"I do when there seems to be reason." Belle rose and went back across the room and stood by the stove.

"What kind of reason does it take?"

"I can't explain."

Once more Cushman felt the frustration and anger against something he could not come to grips with. He was watching Belle gravely when Big John knocked lightly on the door jamb and came in.

He made the perfect focal point of anger. Without thinking, Cushman looked at him and said, "Get out."

"Oh?" Big John blinked owlishly in the light, and then his whole expression hardened. "Is that a challenge, Cushman?"

"I told you to get out of here."

"Both of you stop it!" Belle said.

Big John raised his hand in a smooth quieting gesture. "This seems to be a matter between gentlemen, Belle. If Cushman cares to join me, we'll both step out. I'm sure there's room enough back in the trees to adjust our differences without rousing the whole camp." He took a lantern off a nail on the wall. "If I may?"

Cushman took off his coat and dropped it over the back of a chair. Big John lit the lantern and walked toward the back door. When Cushman stepped out he half expected that the man would try to nail him as he came through the doorway, but Big John was waiting, looking casually toward the trees behind Belle's wagon.

They walked together into the timber until they came to an open place. Big John was huge, all right, and he moved with an easy grace in the jumping light of the lantern. He looked up at the curving limb of a yellow pine over his head and reached up to hang the lantern on a snag.

Cushman wanted to hit him then, but he held off because his act might lose them the lantern and leave them flailing in the dark. The illumination was poor at best and the outer edges of the yellow light were ragged with shadows.

Big John kicked a rotting log out of the way. He started to remove his coat. Cushman struck at him when his arms were encumbered by the sleeves. It was an

accepted, reliable move; you fought to hurt a man, not
to provide a sporting exhibition.

Cushman's blow missed as Big John took one smooth
step backward and pivoted away like a matador. Cushman
went forward off balance and Big John tripped him.
Cushman caught himself on one knee. His hands ploughed
through the rich brown cubes where the rotting log had
lain. He scrambled on ahead to get out of the way of a
kick. When he came to his feet and turned, he saw Big
John calmly finishing the removal of his coat.

Big John hung the garment on a limb snag, and faced
Cushman with his hands at his sides. There was a hot
tightness around Big John's eyes, but his body appeared
perfectly relaxed. Cushman sighted on the big sandy
mustache and the cold eyes above it and went in to beat
Big John down.

The Englishman's hands went up in a classical fighting
pose. Cushman felt like laughing when he saw the move.
He hunched his shoulders and strode in. His head snapped
back and he felt the sharp sting of blows against his mouth.
They were nothing. He had merely to beat aside the silly
position of Big John's arms and get to him.

The plan was simple, but Cushman could not quite
make it work. The arms were always in his way. His
best punches slid off elbows and shoulders. Once he was
sure he had a straight powerful blow well carried, but
Big John's head moved a few inches to one side and the
blow went over his shoulder.

And then Cushman found his left arm neatly trapped.
An instant later a jolting blow took him under the heart.
Big John stepped around him, circling away from his
right hand.

God damn the polished smoothness of the man's methods! Sure, he could give a boxing lesson, but that didn't
count in the long run. Cushman had enough of boxing
lessons. He lowered his head and charged to ram the
breath from Big John's stomach.

Big John hammered the side of his neck with a slashing
blow. His knee came up and crashed into Cushman's
face. With the heel of his hand Big John drove Cushman's right shoulder back and then hit him in the side of
the jaw. Cushman reeled into a tree that kept him from
falling. Without shifting his eyes or the high position of
his hands, Big John kicked Cushman in the knee. It was

just a trifle high or it would have been a crippling smash.

And now Cushman had a lesson, too, in the less polished methods of frontier fighting. Big John had mastered two schools of combat, making a rare and dangerous combination of them.

There was still no doubt in Cushman's mind that he could beat the man. He was dazed and hurt and far behind at the moment; but Big John had not taken any of his punches yet.

He got to Big John with two of his hardest blows a few moments later. He saw Big John's mouth sag and his eyes fog. Cushman tried to finish him then.

There was a hellish cleverness in the arms that were constantly in the way, in the roll and thrust of Big John's shoulders, in the way his head moved just an instant before a blow would have crashed against it, in the way he tied up Cushman's arms when Cushman was in close enough to chop.

A good many times Cushman connected with his solid strokes, but he never could quite get in the clincher. Big John's bristling mustache was smeared with blood. One eye was dropping at the outer corner. But still his fists kept jarring out, rocking Cushman, preventing the one solid moment when he could have both feet set, and a clean shot at Big John's stubborn jaw.

After a time Cushman became aware of the sodden, wearying impact of the punishment he was taking. He was slow. He swung and it seemed that he had power, but when his fists landed, he knew he could not smash Big John down.

With a queer, distant breaking comprehension, Cushman realized that he was losing the fight. He tried harder then. He went down from a blow he never remembered receiving. He saw Big John's legs close to him. A boot came up as if to kick Cushman. Cushman managed to lower his face and put one hand on his head. But the kick didn't come.

Cushman staggered up. Big John was ready. His guard was lower now, his fists not so tautly held. Cushman flailed away at him.

Just when Cushman felt that Big John's strength was crumbling, the man went deep into some source of strength for power that spun Cushman to the ground once more. He rose, knowing he would not have strength to do so again—and Big John knocked him down.

Cushman lay with one arm thrown across the log Big John had tossed aside. He saw his opponent standing with his arms down, his breath all ragged and gusty, his mustache limp with blood and sweat. Cushman imagined himself getting up, going on to beat Big John.

But it never came about. He tried to rise and could not, even when his mind ran ahead of feeble effort and made him think he was getting up. His breath came out through swollen lips. "I'm not licked yet."

But he couldn't rise. Big John stared down at him with a strangely blank expression. Big John tried to walk carefully to a tree. His legs were wobbling, but he lurched to the support of the tree and stood there with one arm hooked over a limb. After a while, as if it weighed a hundred pounds, he raised his hand and began to re-form the straggling shape of his mustache.

Rising slowly, Cushman fell over the log, and lay awkwardly until he could find strength to haul his legs on across the log and get them under him. The sickness of nausea and utter exhaustion was like a cloud around him when he finally rose.

Deep inside there was still a will to fight; but a deeper law of nature told him the futility of trying to reach Big John across the fifteen feet that separated them. Cushman defied the greater law and tried anyway.

He took two steps and fell. He crawled on his hands and knees to reach Big John, feeling the sharp bite of dry pine needles in the raw flesh of his knuckles. He came to Big John and stared up at him like an inquiring dog.

"Here now," Big John said, and bending shakily he reached Cushman's hand and helped him to his feet.

Cushman grabbed a limb. They stood close to each other, staring. All at once Big John's swollen mouth broke into a grin. He tried to laugh. "Somebody should have paid to see us!" he gasped. He touched his face gently. One eye was completely closed now. "No man—I say no man, Cushman—ever hit me like that."

Cushman wondered why his own hatred of Big John had vanished. It was not possible that he could like Big John, but it was so.

They regained strength clinging to the same tree. After

a time Big John retrieved his coat. He looked at the ground where they had fought. "There must have been two stags here. Come on, Cushman, let's go to water on the west fork."

With the lantern hanging on a sluice box they washed their hurts in icy water. The man who owned the sluice came out of a bough hut with a rifle and challenged them, but when he walked closer and saw who they were and their condition, he held the lantern high for them and made no comment.

After a time they walked back toward town together, the lantern throwing blobs of yellow light and leaping shadows before them.

"This won't hurt Dunbar's plans about—" Cushman said.

"Of course not. Don't be an ass, Cushman." The clipped precision of Big John's voice contrasted queerly with his battered face and wild hair. "I've already arranged for Potts and Hardesty to come here and examine the mine. Disrupt an agreement merely because you and I had to settle something that was inevitable? I should say not!"

They walked on across the clearing where they had fought. Big John said, "Will you come over and join me in a drink? It might allay certain unpleasant rumors which are bound to come."

"No thanks."

"You have a grudge?"

"No," Cushman said, "I don't."

"Excellent! I still don't love you as a brother, Cushman, but I've relieved my feelings against you. I was obliged to hate you because Belle was attracted to you, and that was made worse by the fact that you heard me offer her marriage the first night she was here. She refused me. You remember that?"

"I remember."

"That's all," Big John said. "I feel better now. Sure you won't have the drink with me?"

"Yes, I will."

They went in the back door to Big John's living quarters and drank from his private stock. Later, they went out to the bar and had another drink together so that everyone could see them in friendly conversation.

They shook hands when Cushman was ready to leave. "I was refused too," he said.

"I'm damned!" Big John was puzzled. "I wouldn't have believed it."

Cushman went back toward the hut where he and Dunbar and Marvel lived. The climb brought out the full extent of his aches and bruises. His lungs pounded hard against sore ribs. He knew he had been beaten.

Dunbar was drawing a sketch of a smelter on a shaved board. Marvel was in his bunk, smoking his pipe. They stared at Cushman and then they looked at each other.

"Big John," Cushman said.

"Good Lord!" Dunbar leaped up, spilling the shaved board from his knees.

"I didn't hurt anything, not even him. The mine will go right on, Jake."

Dunbar picked up the board and sat down again. He let out a long breath. "What do you mean, you didn't hurt him?"

"You can see me, can't you?"

"Yeah, but there's plenty of Big John to work on. You must have got a piece of him now and then," Dunbar said.

Cushman's grimace was lopsided and painful. "There's a lot of him to hit back, too."

Marvel got out of his bunk. He rummaged around in his duffel bag and pulled out a tin of salve wrapped in a stained cloth. His grandmother in Vermont had given him the salve when he started west. It had melted half a dozen times, but that, Marvel said, had not affected its qualities. It was a special treasure he used only in severe emergencies—and then sparingly. He handed it to Cushman with a rare smile.

"Here, Ed. Spread it on." As an afterthought Marvel added, "Use up what's on the rag first."

CHAPTER SIXTEEN

THEY closed the ends of the trail across the harsh slope of the mountain. From beside the hut in early morning Cushman liked the sight of the Z's scored in hard granite. He knew John Marvel was proud of the trail too, but

Marvel wasn't one to say. To Dunbar it was an already forgotten step toward something much greater.

Both Cushman and Dunbar had sold their property in the gulch, retaining only Dunbar's cabin. Victory was still going strong, but those who knew were aware that returns on all the placer ground were falling off sharply.

With their money going fast, Dunbar wanted quick action on the Illinois. Big John's engineers were coming, but they were slow. Packing ore with horses was slow too, Dunbar said. They needed an aerial tram. By night he drew pictures of one, wearing out shaved boards rapidly.

They stockpiled their ore near the site Dunbar had selected for the smelter. Miners immediately began to carry it away for hand crushing and panning. It was not rich enough to make anyone wealthy by such crude methods, but industrious thieves could net a few dollars a day.

Dunbar considered the stealing good advertising for the Illinois; anyway there was so much ore in the mountain that a few hundred pounds carried away was no loss.

In Victory there were a few canny people who foresaw the end of placering operations—but only a few, for the yellow flakes were still coming from the creeks. Russian Bob saw the handwriting. He sold out quietly on the basis of ill health. Big John began to curtail credit.

Belle Drago was another who observed the slackening. Toward the end of summer there were more miners in Victory than ever before, but the amount of dust and coins dropped three times a day in the iron pot at her serving window began to lessen. She had a blacksmith check her wagon thoroughly, inspecting all the iron work and replacing bolts. She had Ollie Hardwicke, her helper, paint the wagon a dark blue, and she told the Kentons to keep an eye out for a team of four good mules.

These preparations troubled Cushman, and he worried also about the easy, agreeable way Big John continued to pay court to Belle. Big John didn't know when to quit; he had an Englishman's cheerful stubbornness.

Cushman found that he himself could not stay away from Belle, although he had very little to say when he was with her. He was no casual conversationalist like Big John.

They both were sitting in the restaurant one night watching Belle making pies. Big John said, "So you'll go on to another camp, Belle, and go through all the drudgery and insults again. Do you like the prospect of it?".

"No." Belle dropped a thin sheet of pie crust over a pan and trimmed the edges with a small, sharp hunting knife. "Sometimes I hate the sight of men's hungry faces."

The summer had left its marks on her. There was the same expression of strain and wondering in her face that Cushman had seen in the looks of emigrant women when they came into Ruby Valley, grateful for the respite but knowing they had to go out on the desert again.

"But you will go on?" Big John asked gently.

"Yes."

"Why?"

"Money," Belle said.

"I don't believe it," Big John said. "Money buys only one kind of independence. Not that I have any quarrel with money, but it sometimes cuts you away from other things."

"I'll have to take that chance." Belle gave Cushman a swift look and then she said to Big John, "Why don't you ask Ed what *he's* been chasing all his life?"

"He's found it," Big John said. "He and Dunbar will tear the mountains apart. Dunbar will have a hundred ideas at once and Cushman will spend his time stabilizing him and between the two of them they'll have a wonderful time and grow very rich in the bargain."

"I hope so," Cushman said. But he knew nothing was going to be entirely wonderful without Belle.

She was still working quickly and efficiently when Cushman and Big John went out.

Big John looked in on his bartenders and then he and Cushman had a drink together in the saloonman's quarters. The rooms were well furnished and snug; they reflected Big John's background as a one-time gentleman.

"You could say I have everything she needs," he said. He shook his head. "Except myself. She doesn't want me, Cushman."

Cushman picked up a book titled *The History of the Dutch Republic*. He fingered the leather work a moment and put the volume down.

"Part of me still hates you, Cushman," Big John said in a puzzled tone. "That's natural, isn't it? You could have that woman if you worked at it half as hard as I have, but all you do is sit around like a lout."

"I tried."

"Not very hard, I'd guess." Big John scowled at his whisky. "Why should I be a John Alden? I never was a sportsman when it came to losing. When I lost I always wanted to break a cricket bat over somebody's head, instead of smiling and shaking hands. You Americans make no bones about losing hard. That's what attracted me to this country."

Big John poured the drinks again. "Hardesty and Potts will be here toward the end of the week. Sound chaps. If their report is good, we'll all be in for a fortune."

Dunbar was happy to hear the news about the coming of the engineers. "Not that we need them," he said, "but the investors Big John will bring in have to be satisfied." He watched four drillers driving into the mountain through the middle of the great bloom of rich quartz. Six others were enlarging the ledge for building room.

Cushman thought of the slopes, the way they had been bright with heavy snow in late spring. "Might not be ready this winter, Jake. It'll take time to do business between here and England."

"I know, I know. Time is the most expensive thing in life."

Thinking back on the years when he had stood apart from men, Cushman knew that Dunbar was right.

Francis Hardesty and Elwood Potts did not arrive when Big John had said they would; they came a week later having stopped to examine operations at Cache Creek placer a few miles farther up the Arkansas.

They rode into Victory towing a pack horse. They were both young men and at first glance they looked to be only another pair of gold hunters who had arrived too late. Potts was a tall, fair-haired man who seemed to best fulfil the camp's idea of an Englishman. Hardesty was a heavy-set, dark-haired man with a stiff military mustache and an abrupt manner of speaking. Both were friendly, and obviously they knew their way about the mountains.

They stayed with Big John. Their first afternoon in camp, Potts and Hardesty carried water to a wooden tub behind the saloon and stunned onlooking miners by bathing briskly in the icy stuff. Then they changed their clothes and had a dinner with Big John that lasted two hours.

Dunbar was up the mountain and did not learn of the arrival of the engineers until the next morning. He came rushing down. Hardesty and Potts had taken their pack horse and gone hunting. Dunbar was fit to be tied.

"What the hell did they come here for—a summer excursion?"

Big John hid a grin and said, "Slowly, Jake, slowly. They'll be back."

The engineers returned three days later, completely disreputable in appearance and with two large bucks which they referred to as stags in spite of all instruction to the contrary. Hardesty and Potts barbecued the deer over pit fires behind the saloon. That took the best part of a day and night, and after the celebration, which the whole camp attended, the engineers rested for another day.

Dunbar said, "Maybe next winter they'll go up the mountain."

Deciding that they had properly arrived, Hardesty and Potts did go up the mountain. They started at the mine, but examined it only briefly before going higher up. Once they were moving, Dunbar had to admit that they covered ground enough to patch hell a mile. For a week the engineers explored the mountain, going around it and over it, poking into seams and outcrops in a hundred places.

They took another two days exploring the glacial drift below the mountain, examining the twisting hills clear to the valley.

Dunbar was jumping, not so much because he wanted to hear their report, which would do no more than confirm what he was sure of already, but because the opinion would at last get major wheels in operation.

They made an offhand report one evening at the timberline hut when Big John was present. Hardesty, gesturing with a big-bowled pipe, did most of the talking. "We'll prepare the full opinion later," he said, "but here is what it is in common language . . ."

The essence was that the Illinois was no more than a freak bloom of gold-bearing quartz that would not extend to any appreciable depth into the granite.

Dunbar was completely motionless. "What makes you think so?"

"There're certain fracture patterns in the mountain," Hardesty said; "intrusions that indicate the entire structure is of recent origin, and tremendous glacial gouging that has carried away hundreds of feet of the face itself. Some time subsequent to the period of sedimentation the whole region here was high above sea level, and that's undoubtedly when the folding and faulting took place that make it now so difficult to tell—"

"Those are words," Dunbar said. "What I want to know is how you can be sure the gold in the Illinois won't go to the middle of the mountain."

"Impossible," Potts said. "The faulting itself precludes that."

Cushman said nothing. He was not satisfied with what he was hearing; but he couldn't disbelieve simply because the report was bad, and he knew too little of geology to understand everything the engineers were saying.

"Where'd the gold come from that's in the gulch?" Dunbar demanded.

"Probably from glacial action," Hardesty said. "We'll prepare a complete report within a few days."

"I've got about enough of it now," Dunbar said. "You say the Illinois is no good. That's it, ain't it?"

"Yes, I'm afraid so," Hardesty said. He started to explain further, and saw that technical exposition was not what Dunbar wanted. "Commercially, I'm afraid it would not be even a long gamble, Mr. Dunbar."

Dunbar looked at Big John. "You'll take their report on this?"

"It disappoints me, but I accept their word as truth. They're men who know, Jake. They've been all over the world in this business."

"It ain't been proved to me—not yet." Dunbar spoke strongly, but Cushman knew how badly he was shaken.

Hardesty filled his pipe carefully and lit it. "Let me say, Mr. Dunbar and Mr. Cushman, that you are on the right track. It's our opinion that even Cache Creek will never be a truly great success, but not far from there, on the east side of the river, we found indications of gold masses in place, geologically speaking.

"We've no doubt that these mountains, particularly farther northward, will produce huge quantities of minerals long after all the placers are exhausted. You gentlemen are on the right spoor, but my advice is to spend less money the next time on dead work before you establish, as far as possible, the extent of your prospect."

"Thanks." Dunbar smiled faintly. "Well, we're not through with the Illinois yet."

Hardesty shrugged. He left with Potts and Big John soon afterward. Dunbar and Cushman and Marvel sat silent in the hut.

"You can't trust an Englishman too far," Marvel said carefully, after a long time. "And you're dealing with three of them."

Cushman considered the implication. Of course collusion was possible, to make the mine appear worthless. He was pleased at his quickness in dismissing the idea. A few months ago he would have given it long consideration. He looked at Dunbar.

Dunbar shook his head. "I trust Big John. I trust the engineers too, but maybe their judgment is bad. They can't see inside a mountain, no matter what they say." Dunbar shook his head. "Still, they're smart men. I've no doubt of that."

Dunbar sat with his head resting on one hand. Between his feet on the dirt floor lay one of the shaved boards worn to thinness with his planing. He talked stubbornly, but the black edge of doubt was in his words.

Tempered by greater failures than this one, Cushman now sensed that he was the stronger at the moment. Dunbar had given him much. Cushman tried now to return some of the help and faith he had received.

"We'll never know the truth until we look inside the mountain. We're not sure till we do that."

Dunbar raised his head. "A few more weeks will clean out our last dime."

"All right. Let's gamble."

"You're willing to?"

"I want to," Cushman said. "If we get licked there's nothing dishonorable about it. This is only one mountain, too."

"That's what Hardesty said." Dunbar stood up and began to pace the floor. The old look of eagerness and drive came back to his expression.

They spent their dwindling money. They hired men to work the clock around. Between walls of monzonite porphyry the golden face of the Illinois widened to four feet. Aspens and cottonwoods on the watercourses running toward the Arkansas turned golden. A light snow fell and melted in one day, and then there was glorious Indian Summer.

But the mountain sent cold winds slicing early and late when there was no sun. Looking up the granite slopes, Cushman knew that winter was never very far away. With black powder shots they raced the coming of the snows.

Big John came up, looked at the widened face, and was enthusiastic. He offered to supply the partners money if they ran short before they tested the tunnel thoroughly.

The mountain did not take quite all the treasure they had shoveled from the gulch below. It closed them off while they still had a little left. In two days the golden face disappeared. For a while there was a thin streak of quartz, faltering and uncertain, wandering without strong design. Then it died against solid granite which was like nothing they had encountered before.

For another week they fought on. There was nothing but more granite.

Cushman let Dunbar make the decision. Dunbar was a dreamer, but he was no fool. They stood one afternoon on the dump with the crew dismissed for good. Below, the fall-touched valley was long and beautiful with color. Dunbar looked down in silence.

He did not glance back when they began to descend. At the foot of the last switchback Cushman stopped to look up at the long trail they had torn into the mountain. They had nothing to be ashamed of; their failure was honest all the way. . . .

Marvel had his gear packed and was ready to leave. He had waited only to say good-by, which he did gruffly. He slung his pack on his shoulder and started off. "Only one mountain, remember." Small pennants of pipe smoke whipped back across his shoulder as he went down the trail.

Cushman and Dunbar sat in the hut. They had sent the tools, and everything that was of any worth, down with the crew to be stored in Dunbar's cabin in Victory.

"Up the river—up there where the engineers said? Shall we make the next try there?" Cushman asked.

Dunbar studied him. "Not you, Ed. You haven't got your heart in mining. I have, and I'll go on trying. Some day I'll hit. I don't want the money; I want to build things. So do you, but not the same things."

It was true, and yet it was a breaking up that hurt. No matter how closely drawn he and Dunbar had been, Cushman knew they were of different natures and different ambitions. They would always be friends but this one venture together, whether it had failed or succeeded, was enough for them.

"You know what?" Dunbar said. "All we lost was a little money." Suddenly he thrust out his hand and they shook hands, looking at each other gravely. Cushman saw a tough little man who would never be beaten. Some day he would make more than mining history with his dreams. Cushman saw more than that—the man who had given him faith and understanding to live more than a defensive, wary life.

Until after sunset they stayed at the hut, packing their duffel bags, dawdling about with little to say to each other. Dusk was nearing when they started down to Victory.

Cushman was going away, but he wasn't going without Belle. If he had asked her twice to marry him, he had not done so with any show of hope or forcefulness. He had withheld his faith, just as he had worked toward making the Illinois a mine without belief.

Now, because he knew he loved Belle, he would put his heart into his asking. He would win, too.

CHAPTER SEVENTEEN

WHEN Cushman knocked on the door of the restaurant, a man's voice bawled, "Come in!" Cushman stepped quickly out of the sharp fall night into the warmth of the room, keenly aware of his quick pitch of resentment because a man had answered for Belle Drago.

She was there, standing near the serving window. Two men were in the room. One was sitting near the cupboards by the stove, eating a pie which he held in his lap. He glanced up briefly. Cushman made nothing of his face beyond a wolfish leanness and beard stubble.

The second man was sitting before the remains of a meal at the worktable. He reached under a dirty, shapeless

hat to scratch his head as he turned inquiringly toward
Cushman with a bold stare. Thin, purplish lips were set
in a dirty beard, gray-streaked. His nose was small, with a
boneless look.

A shock like a heavy blow against the heart went
through Cushman. Time collapsed as he stared at the
man.

It was Rumsey Snelling. Except for the gray in his
scraggly beard, he looked no different from the day
Cushman had last seen him at Gravelly Crossing.

Rumsey said, "Who mought you be, friend?" His eyes
dropped before Cushman's fixed look.

Cushman heard the beating of the wings of the monster
bird that came in bad dreams to tear Kathy away from
him. For an instant he was no longer a mature man;
he was the scared, desperate boy of long ago. He wanted
to shriek a curse to drive away the vision of Rumsey
Snelling.

But the man was flesh and blood. He moved. He raised
his eyes to look slyly at Cushman. A big, gray-knuckled
hand went out on the oilcloth of the table and toyed with
a fork.

"The cat's got this feller's tongue," Rumsey said. He
looked at the woman standing motionless by the wall.
"Who is he, Lizzie?"

The second shock piled in upon the first. Cushman
looked at Belle. Lizzie . . . Lizzie Snelling?

"This is Ed, a friend of mine," Belle said. She watched
Rumsey with a steady, bitter expression. Without shifting
her gaze, she went on. "This is my father, Ed." She moved
one hand listlessly toward the other man. "My brother,
Reed Snelling."

"Well, howdy there, Ed," Rumsey said with a false
heartiness. He looked slyly from Cushman to his daughter,
as if gauging the extent and nature of their friendship.

Reed looked up and grunted. He frowned, watching
Cushman with a vaguely searching expression for a moment, and then he resumed his eating. Pie juice dripped
as he spooned it up from the pan. He brushed his hand
carelessly where it had stained his pants.

Rumsey said, "We was talking over some business, young
feller, but since you're a friend of Lizzie's, set down, set
down."

Belle's head was high. Cushman saw the desperate appeal in her eyes, and he saw how her body was braced against the wall. There was no place to sit down, and he didn't want to, anyway. He moved past Rumsey and stood with his back to a section of cottonwood log that served as a meat block.

All the anger and bitterness of the lonely years flooded him with their acid. Why hadn't she told him? She could have told him long ago, instead of letting him find out like this. In his mind he yelled out at Rumsey, "You filthy old bastard, don't you remember me? I'm the kid you left to die with his sister on the Humboldt!"

But Cushman said nothing. He looked from Rumsey to Belle and then he looked away.

"Me and Reed have been traveling some," Rumsey said. "Been over a good many states and some places that ain't states. Hell, we seen mining camps that is camps, not some little place stuck away in a hole like this— Give me some more of that there pie, Lizzie. You're just like your ma in some things. She learned you good when it come to baking a pie."

Reed stood up. "You can have the rest of this one, Pa. I guess I overmatched myself, considering what I et for supper." He carried the pie over to his father, who licked the spoon and began to eat.

Belle looked straight at Cushman. Her pride was a high, burning, angry quality, and then it dulled away before his look. Misery came into her face and she wouldn't face him again.

Reed went back to the stove, glancing around with a proprietary air. He kicked the chair around to where he could sit with his feet on the oven door. He belched and pulled a plug of tobacco from his pocket.

"Yes sir, we traveled here and there," Rumsey said. "It was quite a surprise to Lizzie when her old pa and her oldest brother dropped in on her today."

"How'd you find her?" Cushman asked.

"Oh, pshaw!" Rumsey tried to eat and laugh at the same time. Juice ran into his beard and he ducked his head to rub his chin against his shoulder. "We heard she come back this way. People notice Lizzie. Taking a fancy new name didn't fool us none.

"We heard in Denver about a gal up here running a big eating place. That Joe Kent fellow—Kenton?—he knowed all about her. He told us." Rumsey shook his head.

"Lizzie was always up to something. In San Francisco she used to run away to the ships in the harbor. Then she'd be talking about going to some far-off heathen place. She was always listening to wealthy folks talk and copying the way they said things."

Rumsey finished up the pie, tipping the pan to get the last of the juice with the spoon. He pushed the tin away from him and wiped his beard, grinning at Cushman as if the latter's silence meant rapt attention.

"I had to whale the daylights out of her a few times for her queer ways. She had too many fancy ideas for her own good. Once, after her ma died, she even tried to stow away on a ship—and her only fourteen years old." Rumsey shook his head. "When you got a big family to bring up and your old woman plays out and dies on you, you're sort of up against it. I did the best I could— I don't suppose you're a married man, Mr. What was it Lizzie called you? I ain't worth a damn at names."

"Cushman." His own name and the curiously tight sound of his voice ought to bè enough, Cushman thought.

Rumsey tossed his hat on the table. It sprayed a little shower of dust against the light. He ran loose-knuckled fingers through his hair. "Sounds like a name I've heard somewheres, but like I said, I ain't worth a damn on names. Yes sir, I had the devil's own time with the kids. Jeff got himself killed at a sawmill—"

"John," Belle said tonelessly.

"I always get 'em mixed up," Rumsey said. "I grieved for that boy, I'll tell you. No matter how many you got, you love 'em all." He wiped a long finger in the pie tin and licked it. "Lizzie, she run away another time and I found her washing dishes in a place up near Sacramento. She was the beatin'est one for running away." Rumsey grinned at Cushman, as if sharing paternal mirth over the ways of children. His expression added to the crashing sickness Cushman felt.

"A young thing like that, leaving the protection of her pa and her brothers," Rumsey said. He pondered on the ingratitude of his daughter. "The boys grew up and sort of spread out. Me and Reed was just kicking around, sort of looking for Lizzie, you mought say. We was figuring to do some mining when we heard about her being here. That Joe Kent fellow, that hauls freight, he knew quite a bit about her. His brothers wasn't much to talk, but he sure did."

Rumsey got up and stretched. "Like I said, Victory ain't much of a place, but Lizzie done good here. Of course there ain't no need for her to hire help no more. Reed can work a little and I can help out with the money end of things. It ain't much of a camp, but I reckon me and the boy been in worse ones, huh, Reed?"

Reed said, "I guess," and spat upon the floor.

Cushman said to Rumsey, "Is Lizzie your only girl?"

"Yep! Boys was mostly what I had. Me and—"

"You had a baby girl at Gravelly Crossing on the Humboldt River fifteen years ago," Cushman said.

Rumsey stared uneasily at Cushman. "Oh, that one—" His eyes slid away. "How'd you—" He nodded. "Sure, Lizzie's told you about that, huh?" He shook his head sadly. "The baby died on Donner Pass."

"Long before that," Belle said. "At Big Meadows."

Reed's long neck was sticking out of his shirt in a strained position as he looked at Cushman. "Is he one of the fellers that's been trying to marry you, Lizzie. He acts—"

"He's Eddie Cushman." Belle looked at her father. "You took his father's wagon at Gravelly Crossing. You left—"

"No! No!" Rumsey's face turned the color of his hands. "The Indians got that boy and his sister! They was—"

Reed lurched up, spilling his chair. "It *is* him, Pa! I knowed it but it didn't hit me!" He looked wildly over his shoulder toward the back door. He righted the chair and put it between himself and Cushman.

Rumsey fell into his seat at the worktable. He raised both hands in a defensive gesture. "The Indians was coming, Eddie boy. A big bunch of them—"

"We never saw an Indian until we got to the Truckee," Belle said.

"You was gone three, four days, Eddie boy. We waited as long as we dared. God bear me witness, that was the way it was. We—"

"We waited less than twenty-four hours," Belle said.

Rumsey rubbed his hand across his face. "I can't remember, I can't remember nothing clear about it now. All I know is we did everything we could for your poor pa and ma, Eddie. boy. We laid 'em out real nice—"

"You took Ashley Cushman's best clothes that Ma wanted to bury him in. You knocked her down when she tried to stop you. You wanted her to take Mrs. Cushman's clothes, but she wouldn't touch them. She and I put all those things that belonged to Eddie's mother and Kathy in a chest. Ma and I begged you to wait for Eddie and Kathy."

"No! No!" Rumsey cried. "She don't remember right, Eddie boy. She was just a kid. There was Indians around! We had to go on before the snow came!"

"She's lying on us!" Reed said, and his voice held the same whine as his father's.

Cushman stared at the filthy imitations of men. He didn't know what to do. Rumsey Snelling had ruined his life once and now he had returned to do it a second time. When Cushman didn't move, he saw a slyness come to Rumsey's face, the shifty look of something weak and desperate that begins to see a way out of trouble.

Cushman looked at Belle. She had turned away and was staring out the window.

If he stayed, Cushman knew, he was going to kill Rumsey Snelling with his hands. He stumbled out into the cold night. He started up the street with the intention of returning to the hut below the mine, and then he realized that that was another part of his life that was finished. After a quarter of a mile he turned and came back to town.

Dunbar's cabin was dark. Cushman went inside and sat down on the bunk. All he could remember was the evil of Gravelly Crossing. There seemed no way to be free of it.

He was sitting there in the darkness when the door was bumped open and Frank Eddy said, "Hang onto him, Andy, while I light the lamp."

A match flared and steadied into flame. Eddy jumped when he saw Cushman sitting on the bunk. "Hell's fire, man, why didn't you say something?"

Andy Volgamore ducked through the doorway, carrying Dunbar over his shoulder. Dunbar's eyes were closed and he was mumbling to himself, as happily and helplessly drunk as Cushman had ever seen any man. They put him on the bunk. Dunbar sighed contentedly and fell asleep.

"First time I ever saw him like that," Volgamore said. "I'd say he had a right to it, too." He looked curiously at Cushman. "A few drinks wouldn't harm you either right now, Ed."

They were thinking of the Illinois, Cushman knew. He had forgotten it. He shook his head when they urged him to go with them to Big John's to loosen up with whisky.

They went away. Cushman took off Dunbar's boots and pulled the blankets up on him.

An hour later Joe Kenton knocked the door open and came lurching in. His voice was thick with whisky and there was malicious triumph in his expression as he faced Cushman. "She's not so hoity-toity after all, is she, Cushman?"

The steady burning look in Cushman's eyes disturbed Kenton. He dragged a pistol from his waistband. "Her pretending to be a great lady, so much better than me! All she is is common dirt like her father and brother!"

Cushman watched the confused, excited eyes and felt pity for Kenton. It was the natural reaction of a stupid brute like him to tear down whatever he couldn't have.

"Sit there with that whipped pup look on your face, Cushman! Try to tell yourself that I didn't ruin it for you and Big John and every other fool that wants her! I could have lied, or kept my mouth shut, when her old man came around looking for information. I could have been like my brothers. They still think she's something special.

"I fixed her up. I showed the whole world what kind of people she came from. I beat you all."

Cushman kept staring at Kenton. "And now you're sorry that you did."

"The hell I am!" Kenton shouted, but suddenly he looked sick and defeated. He jammed the pistol back under his waistband. He backed up a couple of steps and then he turned and ran into the night.

After a time Cushman went over to Stapp's livery with his war sack and blankets on his shoulder. He paid his bill to a sleepy hostler. "The pack horse is Dunbar's," Cushman said. It was a small gift, but a little something in return for what Sam Hildreth had given a surly boy long ago.

Cushman rode out of Victory, taking the down-river trail through the timber, the way by which Belle had brought in her oxen through the snow only a few months before.

CHAPTER EIGHTEEN

CUSHMAN rode toward the rising sun. He was free again, free of obligations to human beings. He could go where he pleased. Once more he could insulate himself against the hurt of failure and refusal and the risks of friendship. He could go on into loneliness.

She should have told him who she was before he ran into the stunning shock of it himself. He could have taken the blow much better if she had told him, instead of letting him slam headlong, unexpectedly into the truth. Her not telling him was unlike her. Even long ago at Gravelly Crossing she had been the only one of the Snelling brats with guts and decency.

The miles ahead seemed to build compression against Cushman that was like a physical barrier. Back through the years every parting with those who had tried to give him friendship and love had taken something from him. This time it was taking too much.

What if she had told him the truth months ago? She had known who he was, from the first day in Victory. The chances were that during those first weeks when he was developing links to other human beings, if she had told him who she was, he would have scuttled into his shell instantly; and the chances were, also, that she had never thought him strong enough to accept her if he knew the truth.

Cushman stopped his horse. By brooding over Rumsey Snelling he had given the man a power that did not exist. The first time Rumsey had injured him had been beyond Cushman's power to stop. This time was different. He turned around and headed back.

Victory showed no interest in his return. Sluices were working. Miners were going about their business. Smoke was coming as usual from the restaurant stove pipe and the blue wagon was still in the trees behind the building. The sight of it gave Cushman great relief. It seemed that he had been gone a long time.

He got down in front of the restaurant. Rumsey and Reed were talking inside. "Gawd-amighty, Reed, there'd be a pile of murdering work to a place like this."

"We can hire somebody to run it."

"They mought be lazy and no-good. Best thing is to sell it. That's a good wagon too. The cabin ain't much, but it'll bring a little something. You'd figure it would be fixed up a little better, considering how long she was here."

Cushman was pale when he stepped inside. "Where is she?"

Rumsey's adam's apple began to work up and down. "Now, Eddie boy—" He began to back away.

"Where is she?"

"I reckon she rode away real early this morning. She'll be back, though, or else we can find her."

Cushman glanced around the room. Rumsey and his son had slept on the floor. Their twisted blankets were still there, showing boot marks where they had tramped across them while moving around the room. He saw Belle's key chain on a table.

The top of the stove was littered with bark and wood splinters from the fuel they had shoved into the firebox. There was tobacco juice on the floor, dirty dishes scattered on the table. Cushman picked up the long key chain and pocketed it.

He kept staring at the two. His anger began to die and he was no longer seeing men who had injured him, but symbols that had festered in his mind for fifteen years. His silence terrified the two. Reed stood by the back door, ready to leap away. Words came twisting from Rumsey's purplish lips. "Now Eddie boy, no call to get excited. No call to lose—"

"Never go near her again," Cushman said. "Never even think of her as related to you, because she ain't." He did not tell them that he would kill them; they read that in his eyes, although it was not true.

"Get your stuff and get out."

"We ain't got no way," Rumsey whined. "We come here on the freight wagons. We ain't got no—" He gave Cushman another furtive look and said no more.

Cushman drove them down the street. Miners stopped their work to watch. In silence Cushman paced behind the Snellings and they kept glancing back at him, walking a little faster after each look. Reed trotted away and Rumsey hurried to follow him. They disappeared into the trees.

Cushman's anger was not even disgust now; it was pity and with the coming of that his bitterness began to die.

He turned and bumped into Jake Dunbar, who showed the effects of his fearful drunk. Big John was there beside him.

"Where'd she go?" Cushman asked.

"Up-river. We just found out and were getting ready to trail along to make sure she got where she was going without any trouble." Dunbar's blue eyes smiled. "She left after she found out you'd run away."

Big John gave Cushman a heavy look. "So the lout at last got off his backside."

"I don't think she'll want to come back here even long enough to sell her property," Dunbar said. "Big John and me will do that much for her. Where'll you two be?"

"I'll let you know," Cushman said. It occurred to him that the three of them were assuming something that was not yet settled.

Big John put out his hand and he and Cushman stood with a hard grip between them for a moment. Big John was half serious when he said, "I'd rather break your jaw for you, Cushman, you lucky bastard." He spun around and walked back toward his saloon.

Dunbar slapped a poke into Cushman's hand. It had to be, Cushman knew, about the last of his gold; and he knew, also, how much it would offend Dunbar if he refused the present.

"Get out of here," Dunbar said. "She bought one of Stapp's crowbaits, so she won't be too far off."

She was riding across the high valley, going toward Weston Pass. Cushman kept pushing his horse, and then all at once there was no hurry, for he felt guilt about his behavior last night and doubts over whether he could say the right thing now.

She heard Cushman when his horse was close enough for the sounds to carry into the light wind running down the valley. She turned and saw him. She looked ahead and kept riding. Cushman came up beside her, and still she did not stop.

He saw behind her pride and courage, to the misery inside her. He said, "Stapp could have given you a better rig than that."

"I didn't try to bargain."

They rode side by side toward the river crossing where the wind was making pale shadows in the moving grass.

"I told them not to bother you any more," Cushman said. After a time he added, "They won't."

They were at the river when he reached out to the cheek strap of her bridle and stopped her horse. He took the chain with the keys on it and gave it to her. It lay in her hand for a few moments with the fine links piled and shining, and then she turned her palm and dropped it into the tall grass.

"Lizzie."

It was the right word. Watching her face Cushman knew that it carried everything he felt—and could not say: she was Lizzie Snelling, the woman he loved, and her family no longer mattered or could come between them.

He saw her lips tremble and her eyes come alive as she understood everything his use of her right name meant. &

Steve Frazee was born in Salida, Colorado, and for the decade 1926-1936 he worked in heavy construction and mining in his native state. He also managed to pay his way through Western State College in Gunnison, Colorado, from which in 1937 he graduated with a bachelor's degree in journalism. The same year he also married. He began making major contributions to the Western pulp magazines with stories set in the American West as well as a number of North-Western tales published in *Adventure*. Few can match his Western novels which are notable for their evocative, lyrical descriptions of the open range and the awesome power of natural forces and their effects on human efforts. *Cry Coyote* (1955) is memorable for its strong female protagonists who actually influence most of the major events and bring about the resolution of the central conflict in this story of wheat growers and expansionist cattlemen. *High Cage* (1957) concerns five miners and a woman snowbound at an isolated gold mine on top of Bulmer Peak in which the twin themes of the lust for gold and the struggle against the savagery of both the elements and human nature interplay with increasing, almost tormented intensity. *Bragg's Fancy Woman* (1966) concerns a free-spirited woman who is able to tame a family of thieves. *Rendezvous* (1958) ranks as one of the finest mountain man books and *The Way Through the Mountains* (1972) is a major historical novel. Not surprisingly, many of Frazee's novels have become major motion pictures. According to the second edition of *Twentieth Century Western Writers*, a Frazee story is possessed of 'flawless characterization, particularly when it involves the clash of human passions; believable dialogue; and the ability to create and sustain damp-palmed suspense.' His latest Western novel is *Hidden Gold* (1997).